Survival

Carter's Story

The Carpenter Chronicles: Book Four
A Christian Romance

Janice Limb Myers

©2017 Janice Limb Myers and LJM Publishing LLC.

All international rights reserved.

978-0-9861946-4-1 (eBook)

978-0-9861946-5-8 (Paperback)

Cover Photo Credit

shutterstock_196840163

Pixabay.com: Golden Gate Bridge

DEDICATION

For Rachel

Our precious daughter whose mortal life was cut
short before she found her eternal mate.

We loved you yesterday, we love you still,
we always have, we always will.

NOW AVAILABLE ON AMAZON

SURVIVAL-CARTER'S STORY

Book 4 Now In Paperback and eBook

BOOK 1   BOOK 2   BOOK 3

Table of Contents

Prologue

"Thanks, I hope I can live up to it. Now, what's going on?" Peter asked, trying to cover up his concern.

Peter's friendly manner was gone, and he was all business. Carter launched into the whole sorry story yet again. There was silence for a few seconds when he finished, then Peter's clipped tones kicked in.

"It's personal debt, so legally they can't pursue it now that the debtor is no longer living. If we know their identity, we have a strong case against them, not only for trying to illegally pursue debt and for the illegal interest rates, but also for the threats, not to mention running an illegal gambling den in the first place. This isn't a reputable casino; they would have scrapped any marker they couldn't pursue through the courts. It might sound like a lot of money, but to a real casino, it's small potatoes and no great loss to them compared to what goes over those tables on a daily basis. Do you have anything to go on about their identities?"

"Not that I know of; none of the letters were signed. The only thing Kate has actually seen is a strange car hanging about the place."

"Any details on the car?"

"I didn't think to ask."

"Okay, see if you can find out anything at all. I would also suggest you hunt through the deceased's belongings, see if you can find anything relating to the place—a name, an address, what nights they operate, anything at all. Once you've done that, call me right back."

"I will. Thanks, Peter."

"No problem. And Carter?"

"Yes?"

"Stay safe."

"I'll try."

Carter hung up, feeling relieved that another almost-member of his extended family knew the situation and would offer any help he and his father could. There was no doubt that it was a relief to share the burden, despite the guilt for involving them. Having two capable men on his side almost made him optimistic that a solution would be found.

He glanced at his watch, realizing that the minibus he had dispatched to collect the first load of students would be arriving soon. He hurried to the kitchen to see if there was anything he could do to help prepare for their arrival. He'd already helped Kate air out the bunk shed and make up the beds with fresh linens, but there would be a lot of mouths to feed in an hour or two.

Thank goodness, he chose industrial-grade equipment for her new kitchen—they were going to need it! As he entered the room, Carrie was saying goodbye and hanging up her cell phone with a worried expression on her face. Carter placed a hand on her shoulder.

"Everything all right, Sis?"

"Umm, I'm not sure. I've got a confession to make."

Carter sat down across from her at the table where she was seated. "You told Mom, didn't you?"

"I couldn't help it," Carrie wailed. "You know she's got a freaky sixth sense if there is anything the matter with any of us. I tried to put her off the scent, but she badgered it out of me."

"I don't blame you," Carter said, shaking his head ruefully. "I've been avoiding calling her for that same reason. I'd have crumbled too. What did she say?"

"Oh fishcakes, I'm afraid to tell you. Please don't be mad at me."

"I won't, I promise."

Carrie looked guiltily at him across the table. "She's heading out on the next available flight, and of course, wherever Mom goes, Maggie goes, so no doubt Nigel will be with them too."

Carter held a hand out across the table for Carrie to take. "You know what, I was just telling Kate the other day what a blessing it has been all my life always to have my family to rally around when something was wrong, so I either have to be honored to be loved so much or eat my words."

"Then I guess you'd better choose the former," Carrie laughed.

"I just hope I'm not putting you all in danger."

"If anyone is in danger, then we put ourselves there by choice."

"Antonio said the same thing."

"That's my man; I knew I married him for a reason! Besides, the more of us are here, the more we can protect Kate and Josh, right?"

***

Chapter One

Carter Carpenter sat at the table in his sunny, modern kitchen. In front of him, his open laptop displayed the latest email from back home in Utah. His mother, Grace, sent him at least one email a week, and Carter enjoyed saving them for Saturday morning, when he could savor the news and enjoy her bright and breezy style of writing, peppered with dashes of good-natured digs and inherent humor. The emails usually made him laugh aloud and grin sheepishly at any references to his lack of contact. He had to admit he didn't keep in touch as often as he should, but San Francisco was a long way from Utah, the culture even more distant, and San Francisco had become comfortable to him, although he had been back to Utah frequently over the past couple of years.

The large family had seen quite a flurry of activity recently. He'd gone back to attend his eldest sister's engagement party—a glittering affair made all the more newsworthy by the heavily publicized romance between Carrie and Antonio, the former heir apparent of Spain. Then Carter had made another trip home on the pretext of sharing the news that he was nominated for an architectural award for one of his projects. The real reason for the visit, though, was that even before his mother had told him, he had sensed that his twin sister Chelsea was in some sort of crisis. They'd always been close, and the feeling of unease prompted his boarding a plane at the first opportunity.

The email contained some great news. Carter's adopted little sister Courtney was enjoying learning about their faith, and her romance with Peter was still going strong. He had a feeling that it wouldn't be long before he was on a plane again rushing home to another family event to attend another engagement party or maybe even a wedding for his 'little sis' and Peter.

The reunited childhood sweethearts might just skip the formalities of the engagement and go straight for the big day! That would mean out of all the siblings, only he and Cassie would still be single, and he had a feeling that Cassie was so wrapped up in her career as a writer that she had no intention of seeking the traditional route of marriage and children, at least not at present. *Sure makes a guy feel old when even his baby sister may be getting married.*

There wasn't any pressure on him—even less now that the email informed him that Carrie was expecting. That was terrific news; the couple would make wonderful parents, and Grace would be over the moon with her first grandchild. He glanced at the clock on his laptop— 8 am here, but New York was three hours ahead. He grabbed his smartphone and made the call. Antonio's accented tones answered on the other end.

"Hi, Bro, its Carter. How're things?" He could almost hear the smile in Antonio's voice when he responded.

"Things are very, very good, thank you. How are things with you?"

"Oh fine, thanks. I just read the news from home and wanted to call to say, "Congratulations! I hear you're going to be a daddy."

Antonio laughed. "Yes, indeed I am! And I can't wait."

"I can imagine! Anyway, I just wanted to pass on how pleased I am for you guys. I won't disturb Carrie at work; I take it she's still working?"

"Insisting on working right up to the last minute, of course."

Carter grinned, imagining the battle of wills that would cause further down the line. "Of course, she is. Anyway, I have to go into work myself, so I know how it is."

"I'll pass on your message. Thanks for calling! I'm sure we'll catch up soon."

Carter hung up, sat back contently, and looked around him. When he'd accepted the position of Jr. architect at the prestigious Bonham and Lyle in San Francisco, he'd hoped to find some old, sprawling loft apartment that he could renovate himself. To his dismay, most of the apartments that were an easy commute to the financial district where he worked, most had already been modernized to an exceptional standard to fit the young professionals. The outside of his building on 520 Geary may have beautiful Edwardian brickwork with ornate plaster carvings (and boasted an amazing Nychos mural that canvassed one side), but inside, it was sleek, chic, and ultra-modern. In his time here, he'd grown to love the place simply because of the neighborhood surrounding it. Union Square district was the ultimate downtown experience, bursting with art galleries, theaters, restaurants, and bars, as well as the ultimate shopping experience. No one had visited him here yet, but he could imagine how his sisters would react if they were let loose on the streets below. He chuckled at the thought as he gathered up his laptop and left the apartment, soaking in the already buzzing vibe of the place as he walked to his office.

The walk took only twenty minutes or so, and the moderate climate made it pleasant most of the year. Using public transport cut the journey down by only a few minutes and really wasn't worth it. Besides, Carter was sporty and missed the riding, hiking, and climbing he used to do back home. Having little time to exercise, he felt that walking everywhere made up for the lack and allowed him to experience the city to the fullest on a daily basis. The streets were already busy, filled with couples and families making the most of their Saturday.

He had to admit that being the youngest winner of the Cartwright Architectural Award had been a major achievement, but it had its downsides. Clients had flocked to his firm demanding his services, and he found himself working longer and longer hours to spread himself over multiple projects at once. He loved his job and his firm, but apart from

Sundays when he was immersed in his church, he had little time to experience any other side of life apart from work.

By the time he reached Montgomery Street—the Wall Street of the West—the streets were much more quiet. Many of the firms in this area were banks, insurance, and financial firms that were minimally staffed on the weekend. The prestigious address of the high-rise among the Fortune 500 companies as another major coup for Bonham and Lyle. The company had absolutely everything going for it, but Carter still dreamed of having his own business one day. He was approaching twenty-nine now, and he wondered at what age he would feel ready to take that step away from guaranteed clients and the financial security they provided. Still, those were thoughts for another time and place. Right now, he needed to get to his desk and concentrate on his work.

At 4 pm, he slid off his architect's stool and stretched his back and fingers. From his standing position, he glanced over the plans once more, satisfied he had something the client would love. It was time for him to call it a day and go out to experience this great city he lived in and loved.

Chapter Two

Lunchtime on Monday hadn't come soon enough. Despite being in the office at 6 a.m., the day had been crazy so far. Carter didn't often stop for a break, but today he needed to—if for nothing else than to clear his head. He walked purposely from the office, knowing exactly where he was going. Not far down the street was this great little place that specialized in all things grilled cheese. It had a handful of small tables for two tucked in close to the building on the sidewalk. It was Carter's idea of heaven, and he hoped one of the tables would be free.

As he approached, he saw he was in luck—only two of the six tables were occupied. About to claim his space, he was disconcerted to hear sniffling from a nearby table. He glanced over, seeing a young woman with her head bowed over the table and a large handkerchief covering her face.

Most men might have found the sight of a crying woman uncomfortable and awkward and avoided it at all costs, but Carter wasn't most guys. Growing up in a house full of females, he was no stranger to tears, and his instincts to comfort and

19

protect were instantly triggered. He walked the few small steps to her table.

"Excuse me, are you alright?"

"Perfectly fine," she answered sarcastically. I always sit in cafes and cry."

The voice was muffled from behind the handkerchief, and Carter resisted the urge to chuckle at the sarcasm, knowing it would anger her. She hadn't meant to be funny. "Okay, let me rephrase the question. Is there anything I can do to make whatever the situation is better for you?"

The woman raised her head and looked up at Carter with red-rimmed eyes. Recognition flooded his brain as he saw her face for the first time. "Katherine? Katherine Jameson?"

"Peterson. It's Katherine Peterson now," she answered robotically, as if on autopilot. Suddenly, her expression changed. "Holy smoke, Carter Carpenter! What are you doing in San Francisco?"

"I live and work here now. Mind if I take a seat?"

"Oh, where are my manners? Please do. I'm so sorry; I'm all over the place right now."

Carter sat down opposite Katherine, marveling at the chance encounter. He'd met her during the undergraduate architectural program at California Polytechnic State University in San Luis Obispo. She had been the long-term girlfriend of his roommate, Joshua Peterson, and therefore, he'd gotten to know her pretty well. She was around most of the time, and they had often double dated or gone out just the three of them. When Carter got his BA degree early and then moved on to Colombia for his graduate program, he'd initially made an effort to keep in touch with Joshua and Katherine, but as so often happens, life had taken over, and contact had tapered off.

"So, since I'm an old friend and not some random stranger, will you tell me what's wrong?"

"Carter, I wouldn't even know where to start. Everything's wrong. I take it you heard about Joshua?"

Carter frowned. "No, the last contact I had was an invitation to your engagement party, but I was in the middle of finals and couldn't come. How is he?"

Katherine started crying again. "He's dead, Carter. Joshua is dead."

Carter's face went pale. He and Josh were the same age—they'd been roommates and great friends. How could he possibly be dead at such a young age? What on earth had happened? Instead of bombarding her with questions, Carter scooted his chair around so he could place a comforting arm around her shoulders. He gently rubbed her back as she sobbed, waiting for her to cry herself out. It always happened eventually; he knew from experience that patience and understanding were the best he could offer right now. As her sobs turned to sniffles, she wiped at her eyes with the oversized handkerchief again.

"I'm sorry, I'm a mess. You must be embarrassed to be sitting here with me like this."

"Not at all, and you have no reason to apologize. I do think you need to talk about this, though. I think you've been bottling everything up."

"There isn't anyone I can talk to about everything that's going on."

"There's me," he offered with a question in his statement.

Carter caught the flicker of hope in her emerald green eyes as she glanced up at him. Seeming to reconsider, she shook her head. "We haven't been close for years. Why should I burden you with my troubles?"

"Isn't that the testament to a great friendship? One where you can be out of touch for ages then as soon as you see each other, you pick up right where you left off as if no time has passed at all?"

"Yeah, I guess so," she said, twisting the handkerchief around her fingers, unsure of the situation, unsure of him, unsure of life in general right now.

Carter stole a furtive glance at his watch, disappointed to find he'd been out of the office almost an hour already. He didn't want to leave her, but he had no choice—he had an important client meeting this afternoon and still had some preparations to make for his presentation. "Listen, do you live nearby? Can we meet up later?"

"I live out in the bay area, by Livermore Valley. I was only in town for yet another pointless meeting with my lawyer."

"Can you stick around until I finish work?"

"Not really. I've got to be home to pick my son up from school."

"Your son? You and Josh have a son? That's terrific! So when and where can we meet up?"

Carter could sense her inner turmoil, her longing to talk combined with her reluctance to be a burden. She wasn't quite convinced yet that their friendship could be renewed so easily after all this time. He gave her his best puppy dog look—one sure to capture any girl's heart. "Please? I don't want to lose touch again."

"Well...okay, how about Friday? That's the easiest night to get a sitter, so I could come back into the city then."

"No, I don't want to put you out or take you that far away from home. I'll come to Livermore, although I don't know much about the Tri-Valley area. Give me a place and a time, and I'll be there. Google Maps hasn't failed me yet," he grinned, trying to lighten her mood.

He entered the name and address of the restaurant she gave him into his smartphone and promised to be there at 7 p.m. "It was great to see you again, even though I wish it could be under happier circumstances. I'll see you on Friday."

She gave him a weak, watery smile before he stood and headed back to work, resisting the urge to glance over his shoulder all the way. As soon as he was back in the office, he postponed work for five minutes while he typed Joshua Peterson's name into his search engine. The headlines leaped onto the screen, and he wondered how he had missed this story; it was big news. The suicide of a local vineyard owner had made every local newspaper in the Bay area.

For a second, he doubted this could be the same Joshua Peterson he'd known. They'd been studying the same major, and owning a vineyard seemed about as far away from architecture as you could get. As he scrolled further down one of the articles, there was no doubt. The line that Joshua had left behind his wife, Katherine Jameson Peterson, and a son, Joshua Jr., confirmed it.

The picture of the smiling young man at the end of the article tugged at Carter's heartstrings. He had no idea that his friends had lived that close to him all this time. Nor had he any idea that life had gotten so bad for the once happy-go-lucky beach bum he remembered. He wished he'd known. There might have been something he could do, however small, to ease whatever burdens had led the man to take his own life.

With deep regret, he closed the browser and turned his attention to his project.

Chapter Three

Since his arrival in San Francisco, Carter had never bothered to purchase a car. Everything he could possibly want was either on his doorstep or a short walk, tram, train, or bus ride away. He'd explored the city, but he didn't have much interest in the wine-growing regions of the Tri-Valley area. Now he couldn't decide whether to rent a car or buy one.

Deep down, he wanted to buy one in the hope of using it frequently to visit Kate, but he had to be realistic. There was a chance it would just be used this once, then remain untouched for months or years. No, renting one for the weekend was the sensible plan. He did some quick research. The company with the highest rating for customer service was about half a mile away, so easily within walking distance, but they closed at 6 pm. He would need to leave work pretty early to make it.

After making the call and booking the car, he tried to settle down to work. Images of Josh and Katherine together danced through his mind, distracting him. At 4 pm, he gave up and went to tell his boss he was heading out for the weekend, then packed up his laptop and other items he usually carried home with him just in case the evening was a disaster and ended early. Jeannie, the administrative assistant, looked over at him with disappointment.

"Leaving early today, Carter?"

"Yes, there's something I need to take care of before the place closes at 6 tonight."

"Oh, for a minute there I thought you might have a hot date."

Carter grinned at her cheekily. "Well, maybe I do and maybe I don't, but a gentleman never tells."

He sauntered out of the office, laptop bag flung over his shoulder, totally oblivious to the wistful look of longing that followed him out the door. He headed home to drop off his gear and change. Dumping his stuff on the kitchen table, he suddenly had a thought. Heading for the tiny square-as-a-box room that was meant to be the second bedroom, he opened the wardrobe and pulled out a box marked "college." Rifling through the mishmash of items it contained, he pulled out a handful of old print photographs. Skimming through them, he found the one he remembered most clearly. They were attending a rock concert in LA but had headed over early, spending the day exploring the boardwalk at Venice Beach. They were all dressed down for the concert, and Kate stared out of the picture at him, her emerald green eyes shining with excitement, her long auburn hair flowing out around her in the breeze. She was wearing pale faded jeans and converse shoes; her outfit finished off with the tour t-shirt of the band they were going to see later. She looked so different from the red-eyed woman in the business suit with her hair scraped back into a tight bun that he ran into a few days before.

Josh stood beside her, a native Californian surfer dude, his messy, dirty blond hair sun-streaked with natural highlights. His easy, laid-back smile and deep golden tan put him right at home among the beautiful people on the boardwalk. Carter was instantly transported back to that day—the fun they'd shared having caricatures drawn by a street artist, watching men showing off at the local muscle beach, admiring the rollerbladers and skateboarders as they sped along, expertly weaving their way through the crowds.

There was so much to see and do, from the cool to the kooky, and Josh had a great time playing tour guide for them. Although Katherine was also a native Californian, she came from the northwest and hadn't experienced the beach lifestyle before attending the university. Her home, Trinity County, was rugged and heavily forested, more suited to hiking, mountain biking, and river rafting than sunbathing and surfing. She and Carter were thrilled at every new little thing throughout the day, much to Josh's amusement.

Carter was suddenly furious with himself. Why had he let his friends drift out of his life the way he had? They had been so close for a while, and he had practically forgotten about them. What could have gone so wrong in their lives that things had come to this? He couldn't make up for the past—nothing he could do could bring Josh back—but he could certainly try to atone by helping Kate through this any way he could. Heading to his bedroom to change, he took the picture with him, stuffing it into his back pocket when he dressed. Glancing at the clock, he saw it was time to head out and pick up the car before he ended up without wheels for the night.

After signing the forms and leaving with the keys, he wondered what he was going to do next. According to his GPS on his smartphone, the journey to his destination would take forty-five minutes, and he had a little over an hour to kill before meeting Kate. He didn't want to go home; he couldn't even remember if his apartment came with parking or not, it had been so long since he'd read the terms of his lease. He decided to spend a little time just driving around the city—something he'd never done before. It kept his mind occupied for a while, but when he began to grow anxious about the meeting, he decided to head on out to Livermore Valley, where there would be less traffic and more peaceful surroundings.

In the end, he was glad that he did. Preoccupied with how things would go with Katherine, he missed a few turns on the way, and his GPS had to recalculate his route several times to get him back on track. He was only fifteen minutes early when he finally pulled into the restaurant parking lot. Disconcerted to find his heart beating a little faster than it should, he walked in to find Katherine already there. She smiled as she spotted him, but it was a sad, rueful smile. He strode over and gave her an awkward hug before sitting down.

"Hi! I'm glad you made it. Everything fine with the sitter?"

"Yeah, no problem. Lucy's very reliable, and Josh, Jr. knows her well."

The opening conversation was strained, and Carter desperately wanted to put her at ease. "So tell me about Josh Jr.. How old is he?"

"He's six, be seven later this year."

Carter groaned internally. This felt like pulling teeth. He'd thought a mom would be delighted to have an opportunity to talk about her child and the information would flow, breaking the tension. He tried again. "So he goes to school here in Livermore?"

A curt nod and a refusal to meet his eyes was all that he received in return. He changed tactics. "I hope this doesn't upset you, because that's surely not my intention, but I came across an old picture of you guys. Would you like to see it?"

Katherine held out her hand, and Carter couldn't help but notice that it trembled slightly. He dug the picture from his pocket and handed it to her. She took it and stared at it in silence. Finally, a smile crossed her face.

"I remember that day; we went to Venice Beach before the concert. Do you remember that guy with the panther face? We thought it was face-paint and asked where he got it done, thinking we could turn up at the concert with our faces done, too. Remember how shocked we were when he pointed us to a tattoo studio?"

Carter laughed. "Yah, I'd forgotten all about that."

Memories from the day flowed and the ice shattered, the two falling into the easy companionship they had shared back then. They barely remembered ordering or eating their meal; they were so lost in reminiscing about the good times they'd had. The conversation sobered a little when it turned to Josh.

"So, what made Josh change his mind about being an architect?"

Katherine picked up her glass of red wine and took a tiny sip. "I don't know. I'm not sure if he was ever serious about it in the first place if Josh was ever serious about anything. You know what he was like; he preferred having a good time to studying."

"So, he never graduated?"

"Oh, yes, he did manage to do that, and he was talking about it, looking at positions, discussing the pros and cons of the locations and things, but it trailed off after a while. He started going out with his friends more and more, leaving the wife at home. The next thing I knew, he came home one day and announced he'd bought the vineyard."

"Wow, that must have been a shock."

"It was, but he soon brought me around to the idea in the way that only Josh could. He talked about how great it would be to raise our children away from the cities, having all that space and freedom for them, how great it would be being our own bosses and being self-reliant. He made it sound like a dream life, and soon I was as enthusiastic as he was about a life on the vineyard."

Carter nodded. "That's good. So do you still love it as much?"

Katherine's eyes grew watery, and Carter mentally kicked himself for whatever he'd said that had upset her yet again.

"I did, and I thought we were doing okay. I thought we were making a go of it. We didn't know anything about it at first. It was hard work, but we devoted every second to learning, and there was already a great team there who helped us out so much. We were producing wines that were getting great local recognition, and we were slowly building our reputation and expanding our customer base. It was only when

Josh…was gone…and I had the first meeting with the lawyers that I found out we're broke. I mean, I'm broke. Worse than broke—up to my eyeballs in debt, and I haven't the first clue as to how the vineyard will survive.

"Of course, Josh had insurance, but the life policy was void because it was suicide and the policy was less than two years old. I guess we didn't pay attention to the time limit in the policy because I never thought either of us would commit suicide. I thought the key man insurance we bought for the business would still apply, but they're saying his manner of death nullifies that, too, and that there was no special provision for that. I'd just found that out when we ran into each other the other day."

Carter reached over and placed a hand over hers. "I'm so sorry to hear all that, but there must be something. What about a bank loan until you can work your way out? If the vineyard is doing well…."

Katherine was already shaking her head. "Everything is in arrears, and Josh had already taken out a second loan against the business. They haven't mentioned foreclosure yet, but they're building up to it. I get letters practically every day from the bank and other creditors. I've already had to let most of the staff go, and without them, I'll never manage the next harvest on my own, which means no wine to sell in the future. I'm about to lose everything, Carter. I don't know how Josh, Jr. and I will ever survive this."

Katherine was fighting back the tears, and Carter could understand why. Losing a husband so young was bad enough, but being left a widow with a young son and a failing business must be devastating. He racked his brain. "I know it might be a tough decision, but what about selling?"

Katherine swallowed hard, lowering her eyes. "With the books so bad, it would be almost impossible to find a buyer. And even if I did manage to get a buyer interested, the vines will have already died because I can't take care of them by myself. I won't be able to pay off even half the debt with the sale, the bank would take it all, and I'd still owe them and all the creditors."

Carter got the distinct feeling that there was something more to this, something she wasn't telling him. He couldn't figure out what it was, though, and he didn't want to push. Their friendship was still tentative and fragile. She would tell him when she was ready. He felt the overwhelming need to solve all her problems for her in one fell swoop.

For a second, he was back in the family room of the Carpenter homestead, rolling his eyes at his sisters as they gasped in awe at the fairy godmother on the TV screen waving her magic wand and wiping away the troubles and worries of the fair maiden with one magic-filled swish. He could do that. Not only did he make an excellent salary that he barely touched after rent, utilities, and essentials, but his father had also left him and all his siblings a substantial inheritance. His had been invested and stored away in various high-interest accounts since he'd received it eight years before, and he was quite sure the original million dollars was at least five times that now. Added to what was in his regular accounts, he was sure it would be enough to take the place of that magic wand, no matter how much trouble the business was currently in.

He was about to open his mouth and blurt that out, then stopped himself. No matter how close he and Katherine had once been, there was a distance between them now. She didn't know that she could trust him and might see the offer as sinister or charity. He knew she was a proud woman; she would turn him down flat. No, he needed to be smart about this, and cautious. He would have to regain her trust, and he would have to present it as a smart business proposal where they both gained equally. He needed to put a lot of thought into it. Catching himself, he chided himself on his thoughts. That money was his father's legacy to him—it had been earmarked for when he was ready to start his own firm. Why would he suddenly think about giving it away without a moment's hesitation? He was being ridiculous.

"I need to get home," she said suddenly. "If I'm any later, the sitter will be on to double time."

Katherine's words brought him out of his convoluted thoughts. He signaled for the check as she finished her small glass of house wine. Walking her to her car, he asked if they could do this again.

"I don't know…sitters are expensive, and Josh is still fragile right now. Leaving him was hard tonight."

"I understand that. I was hoping we could maybe do something next Saturday afternoon and I could meet him."

Katherine looked at him, obviously wondering what was behind his offer. Carter had wanted to suggest tomorrow but knew it was too much too soon. She would panic and flee, and he might never see her again. Somehow, that thought filled him with a sense of loss. He held his breath, waiting to see if she would agree, trying to keep the pleading expression from his face and his stance casual. He could almost see her mind ticking, wondering if it was a good idea to bring a stranger into her son's life right now. She seemed to come to an inner decision, giving a little nod.

"Sure, there's a great fondue place here that Josh loves. I'm sorry I'm not comfortable with you coming to our home yet. But we could meet for a couple of hours there if you like?"

"Did you say fondue?"

"Yeah, why?"

"Bubbling bowls of melted cheese," Carter groaned, imitating being in ecstasy. "My idea of pure heaven!"

"You and Josh, Jr. both," Katherine laughed, ending the night on a pleasant, relaxed, easy moment as they exchanged numbers and email addresses, promising to firm up the details later in the week.

Carter watched her drive away, waiting until her taillights were gone from sight before getting into his rental. On the drive home, he tried not to focus on why he was so happy, or why he was so determined to be in Katherine's life and become her knight in shining armor, rushing to her rescue. He brushed it off as guilt for failing his friends all those years ago. What he did decide to do was hunt out his rental agreement as soon as he got home and check to see if it included parking; he was definitely going to need a car of his own.

Chapter Four

Carter rose before dawn on Saturday morning, bypassing his usual relaxation time in the kitchen catching up on the family news. He headed straight into the office, giving a cheery greeting to the grumpy night watchman who gave him access to the main building. He worked for six hours straight, making up for the lost time and getting a head start on his schedule for next week. He called to order in for lunch at his desk and spent the time researching cars. He'd always imagined that the first car he would buy here, if any, would be something classic, fun, and fast, like the Dodge Viper he had sitting in the garage of the homestead in Utah. Now he was looking for something completely different. He wanted something safe, reliable, and spacious. In other words, he was looking at family cars.

His rental agreement had indicated he actually had the use of two parking bays in a secure underground lot only a few minutes' walk from his building. So with that problem solved, there was nothing holding him back except his lack of knowledge in this particular area. In the end, he decided on the one that had won several safety awards recently: a Land Rover

Discovery Sport. It was big enough to hopefully impress a young boy while not being so flashy that it would be off-putting to the mother.

He told himself the SUV would be handy if he ever decided to take a road trip home sometime, ignoring the image that flashed through his head—Katherine in the passenger seat and a miniature version of Josh in the back next to an infant strapped into a safety seat. He had no idea where that came from and didn't want to dwell on it. Searching for dealers, he found several in the city, but his heart gave a little stutter when he saw that there was a large one in Livermore. It seemed like the perfect excuse to take a drive there. Packing up, he headed home to pick up the rental he still had after extending the weekend lease and headed off to the Valleys.

In the small but sprawling town, the dealership was easy to find. After completing the deal and being assured the car would be delivered to his workplace the following week, he found himself wondering what he was really doing out here. Telling himself he was curious about the wine-growing region he'd never explored, he took a slow, meandering drive. He had to admit his previous lack of interest was a huge mistake; the scenery was breathtaking, with gentle, undulating hills rolling across the landscape, rows and rows of vines standing like sentinels in the fields nestled within the mountain ranges. It was beautiful and serene, and he could see why it was such an appealing place to live.

He could hardly believe he was only about an hour out of the city. He couldn't help but grin when he saw the large wrought iron gates with the name Pine Valley Winery molded from the metal in a large arc. He recognized the name of the company from the articles he'd read and knew this was Katherine's business. He desperately wanted to drive in to the winery and pay a visit, or at least pull over and learn all he could about her place, but he felt vaguely guilty, like a stalker. Resisting his urges, he drove on slowly, enjoying the stunning views. Maybe one day he would receive an invitation to tour the place, and until then, he just had to be patient.

Arriving back in town, he considered going into the office but decided instead to head home. *I've done enough work for a Saturday.* He sat at his kitchen table, enjoying the warmth of the sun on his shoulders through the large window. Suddenly he felt the need to talk to someone.

Carter never liked to admit that occasionally, when watching all the families enjoying the city, he felt lonely and even a little lost sometimes. He had a large family and missed them all a lot. Despite his preoccupation with work, there had recently been a sense of something lacking in his life, and he was at a loss for how to fill it. There were a lot of nice girls at his church, and he enjoyed the teasing banter and mild flirtation with them. He'd been on a few dates, but he hadn't found anyone that he'd wanted to pursue a relationship with yet. He didn't agree with having a girlfriend just for the sake of it, and he didn't think it fair to lead someone on if he wasn't serious. The few fun Saturday nights he'd had were more about friendship and companionship than romance.

Pushing aside the lack of love in his life, he turned his attention back to his family. He really wanted to call Grace, his mother, and get her take on the situation with Katherine. He knew she would be full of concern and sympathy for the young widow but would advise caution at getting involved in her business affairs and financial situation. Of course, he also had to consider the fact that the business was a winery. Since drinking alcoholic beverages was against his religion, what would his church make of him investing in a business that profited from the making and sale of alcohol? That was something that would need as much careful consideration as everything else. He definitely needed to talk this over with someone.

Deciding he'd better read the latest email from his mom before making the call, he opened up his laptop. Reading the message, he found it to be bright and breezy, but something felt off. It was a little too blasé and full of superficial news, not his Mom's usual style at all. Something was concerning her, and she was keeping it from him. Picking up the phone, he dialed home.

"Carpenter residence."

"Hi Maggie, how are you?"

The voice on the other end of the line warmed, and he could hear the smile. "Carter, good to hear from you! I'm as well as these old bones will let me be."

Carter laughed at the long-term housekeeper who had helped raise him. "Nonsense, Maggie, you're as fit as a fiddle and as sprightly as a spring chicken."

"Don't I wish! I take it you're looking for Grace?"

"Yes please, if she's around."

"She is. Hang on, and I'll get her for you."

There was a moment's silence before his Mom's refined tone came on the line. "Carter, how good of you to call."

"Hey Mom, how're things?"

"Oh, fine. How's life in San Francisco treating you?"

Grace's quick answer and attempt to change the subject confirmed his suspicions. "Come on Mom; I can tell something's wrong. What's up?"

Grace sighed, then gave up the pretense. "I didn't want to worry you, but its Carrie. Antonio had to rush her to the hospital a few days ago."

"Oh no, is she okay? What about the baby?"

"She's stable for now, and the babies are fine. It wasn't a miscarriage like they feared."

"Oh, thank goodness. Wait a minute, did you say, *babies?*"

His mother chuckled. "They just found out it's twins. So much for it skipping a generation."

"That's terrific!"

"Well, maybe and maybe not. The doctors have said that her bleeding was an early warning sign. It's going to be a difficult pregnancy, and they want her to reduce her activity already. She's only four months along, so it's early to be having problems. Her blood pressure is high, and she's developed gestational diabetes. They have things under control for the moment, but it could all cause problems later on, like pre-eclampsia or premature birth. I guess we should be glad she made it through that first trimester—that's usually the turning point. It's why many women don't tell anyone until after that stage, just like Carrie."

"Oh, poor Carrie, I can't believe it."

"I know, we're all devastated for her. Carrying your first child should be a joy and a blessing, not a constant worry. Of course, Carrie being Carrie, she wants to continue working, even if she has to do it from home with her feet up."

"That doesn't sound sensible; being a reporter is a high-stress job. I think it's time for her to quit."

"So do I, but try telling her that. She fought hard to prove herself on the job, and she doesn't want to let it all go."

"I can understand that, but she wouldn't have gone back to work after the birth anyway, no matter how much she told us all she would."

Grace chuckled. "Sometimes, Carter, people need to find these things out for themselves."

"True, she did inherit your stubbornness, after all."

"Careful! You might be grown up, but you're never too old to be put across my knee."

Carter laughed, knowing it was an idle threat. Neither of his parents had ever raised a hand to their children and never would. "I won't call and disturb them, but give them my love when you speak to them. I'm assuming you're in constant touch?"

"On a daily basis," Grace assured him. "Did you call for any specific reason? Anything you want to talk about?"

"Nothing at all," Carter replied. "Just wanted to touch base with everyone."

Ending the call, Carter sighed. There was no way he could involve anyone in his little drama at the moment. It paled into insignificance when the lives of his nieces or nephews were on the line. *Yep, I guess I'm on my own!*

Chapter Five

The weekend took forever to come around again. Carter couldn't remember the last time he'd looked forward to a weekend so much. Katherine had called mid-week to firm up the arrangements, and every night since then, he'd had to resist the urge to call her and chat. He'd gone as far as pulling up her name from his list of contacts and staring at it several times before hitting exit and laying his phone down. She seemed to be occupying his thoughts more and more, and he found it confusing.

They had been close and had enjoyed each other's company very much since they had so much in common, but he had never looked at her in a romantic way. She was his best friend's girl, and that was that. Now she wasn't. She was still a grieving widow with a world of problems, though, and he felt annoyed at himself for complicating matters by feeling a growing attraction for her. He should be there for her as a friend and a friend only. With the decision made to push aside his selfish feelings, he looked forward to the lunch meeting for what it was—a fun afternoon out.

Arriving at the place, he saw her car was already there. Even if Katherine hadn't been sitting beside him, he would have recognized Josh Jr. instantly. He felt his heart lurch as he looked at the tousled blond locks, golden skin tone, blue eyes, and cheeky smile that was currently directed at his mother. He was sure that if he saw a childhood photograph or could step back in time, his old friend would have looked exactly like this at the same age. He walked to their table and stood awkwardly, unwilling to interrupt their moment.

Katherine noticed him. "Carter, hi, good to see you. This is my son, Josh, Jr. Josh, this is Carter, a friend of your dad's and mine from our university days."

"Hi, Katherine, hello Josh, nice to meet you. I hear you recommend the food here?"

The boy squinted up at him, then seemed to accept him into the fold. "Uh huh. It's just the right gooiness. I wanted to order, but Mom said we had to wait for our guest."

"I'm sorry I kept you waiting, but I'm here now. I'm glad it's the right gooiness—that's really important when it comes to fondue!"

"It is," the small boy nodded seriously. "If it isn't, you don't get the right meltiness and stringiness."

Katherine laughed. "Josh, please stop making up words. Carter, take a seat."

Carter sat down at their table while Josh protested that there weren't enough words in the dictionary to properly describe the perfect melted cheese, so he *had* to make them up. Carter chuckled at the boy's enthusiasm.

"All this talk of meltiness is making my mouth water. I'm famished. Shall we order?"

Josh's face brightened, and Carter grabbed the menu, opting to ignore the entrees and salads. After consulting with his companions, he ordered three different cheese fondues and asked for a large variety of items to dip. He had to admit that fondue with a six-year-old was probably the worst date ever to try to impress a girl; but it was a great one for chaos and laughter. They fought each other to be the first to try each dip, dropped things from their sticks, and attempted to guide the dripping strings of cheese into their mouths. Carter knew their behavior was causing some raised eyebrows and the occasional sniff of disapproval from the wait staff, but the clientele around them was watching their antics with smiles on their faces. Heck, he hadn't had so much fun in a long time. With the meal over and everyone thoroughly stuffed, he left a big tip to compensate for their slightly rowdy behavior, hoping it would ensure they were welcome to come again.

Reaching the cars, he was delighted when Katherine hesitated, seemingly as reluctant to bring the afternoon to a close as he was.

"Have you ever had a tour of a winery?"

"No, I can't say that I have," he grinned at her.

"Would you like one? I mean, would you like to follow us back and see the place?"

Katherine seemed nervous, unsure of the invitation. Carter was quick to accept before she could change her mind. Following her along on the road, he felt a flutter of excitement at the thought of spending more time with her, and in such an intimate setting as her home environment. Pulling in between the huge iron gates he had seen a few days before, he found himself on a well-maintained road that led up to two identically stunning houses. Pulling in behind where Katherine had stopped her car, he got out to hear Josh asking if he could go to find Julian. He didn't know which direction to look first as the boy dashed off across the grounds. The place was huge—sprawling, even. There was so much to take in. Katherine moved to his side.

"I see you've noticed the two houses. The place was owned by brothers, and they both wanted to live on the property. The story goes that to keep the wives from comparing and complaining, they built the same houses side by side. It meant that neither of them had a bigger plot, a better house, and so on and saved any arguments."

"Sounds like they knew their wives well! Have you thought of renting out the second one to generate some income?"

Katherine sighed. "That was our plan. With such great staff already in place, we decided we would have the time to do tailor-made holidays. We could offer accommodation, meals, and excursions—you know, tours of wineries, trips into the city for sightseeing. The more the person wanted to be included in their vacation, the higher the rates would be. The houses are structurally sound and in good condition, but inside they're dreadfully dated. We'd started doing up the guesthouse side one room at a time, then the money just seemed to run out, and Josh grew more and more distant, and things just fell apart."

She turned from him suddenly, feigning interest in the landscape around her, but Carter didn't fail to notice the tears in her eyes or the catch in her throat. His heart went out to her, hearing about the plans she had made with her husband, the willingness to work hard with a good business premise to make a successful future for themselves. The idyllic setting, the multiple winery tours to offer, the perfect microclimate created by the valley, and the amazing city of San Francisco with all its tourist attractions nearby would certainly have a wide appeal. The idea of having a personal tour guide to cater to your needs and drive you around while on vacation would also appeal to all those who wished to sample the wineries in the area. If the idea had come to fruition, it would have been a real money-maker. Carter's mind was whirling with ideas, but he suppressed them, biting his tongue and staying silent, allowing Katherine to compose herself. She turned back to him with a smile that was merely a shadow of the ones he used to see from her in their college days.

"Come on; I'll give you a tour and stop at the tasting barn."

"I'd love the tour, but I'm afraid I'll have to pass on the tasting."

Katherine looked surprised. "Oh, you mean you're still a Mormon after all this time? Still sticking to all the rules?"

"I sure am. My faith is still one of the biggest parts of my life," Carter shrugged. "Why does that surprise you?"

"I suppose it shouldn't have," Katherine mused. "I guess just living in the city must be filled with so much temptation to stray that I figured it would be hard for anyone to remain perfect."

"I'm not going to lie and say it's always easy, but it's definitely the right choice for me. How about you? Do you still go to church?"

"I do, it's still a big part of my life too, although as you can tell by the glass of red I had at dinner the other week, I'm not exactly temple-worthy nowadays."

They continued to talk as they walked toward the large stone structures set away from the houses. "So what does the church make of you running a winery?"

Katherine laughed ruefully. "It's not something they're going to have to worry about for much longer, is it? To tell you

55

the truth, there were a few grumbles from some of the older members, the traditionalists. I guess it's a hard one to reconcile, making a profit from something that we consider taboo—not that I am at the moment, but you know what I mean. Mostly, though, the members of my ward looked at it as part of life around here, and that hard work, dedication, and initiative should always be supported and rewarded, no matter what the business. I guess there must be a lot of less-than-ethical professions out there that members of the church are involved in. We just have to find a way to maintain our standards and morals within that profession and apply our particular tenets to every aspect we can. It can be hard to find the balance, but we can't shut ourselves away from the world as it is now; we have to live in it and deal with it. Believe me, when Josh first suggested the idea to me, I spent hours praying for guidance on it, only to find out he'd already purchased the winery! So, I prayed even harder we could survive."

Carter smiled. This was exactly the type of debate and conversation they used to have well into the wee hours of the morning back in the dorm room while Josh lay passed out on his bed from one too many beers. He hadn't realized how much he missed sharing philosophical discussions with someone close. Katherine had always been insightful and intelligent, and the fact that she shared his faith meant they always had something to discuss in depth.

"This is our tasting room and store," Katherine informed him as she led him into a large barn-like space where shelves filled with bottles occupied every wall. Large barrels dotted the place, and a few had been set up as rustic tables with bar stools around them. Halved barrels planted with greenery added a natural touch to the décor. The stone building was deliciously dark and cool, a pleasant relief from the mid-August heat outside.

"This is where people can buy bottles or crates of the wines if they enjoy the ones they try. Here, I'll uncork a bottle. You can just sniff it and check out the bouquet, or if you're feeling brave, do it the proper but snobby way and rinse it around a bit and spit it out."

"I'll stick to the sniffing part," Carter said as he slid onto a bar stool and accepted the glass from Katherine. "I'm sure I'm fine appreciating a nice aroma, but I'm not so sure about the rest. I might even decide I like it!" He gave her a cheeky wink, and they laughed, happy in each other's easy company.

Chapter Six

Carter lay in bed with his hands tucked behind his head. His mind was so full of memories and thoughts of the day that sleep had been eluding him for hours. After the tour of the buildings, Katherine had shown him the houses. They were large, white structures with three stories and an open balcony along the front of the main house. Carter marveled at the French Creole architecture, so unusual for the local area. Inside, Katherine seemed embarrassed by the fact that her own house hadn't been touched for years. Carter had to admit that while some of the mismatched old furniture was interesting, the décor had brought a grimace to his face. The guesthouse was in far better shape, with the majority of the rooms having been modernized already. Only the top floor remained untouched, and it was completely devoid of furnishings.

After touring the buildings came the trip through the grounds, where Carter had met Julian, a single man so dedicated to the vines he'd begged to stay even though Katherine could barely afford to pay him. He was in the process of teaching little Josh everything he could about them, sure that things would work out for the family. He loved the vines so much he claimed they spoke to him, whispered their needs to him on the gentle summer breeze. Carter liked how in touch with nature Julian was; he felt the same whenever he left the city and returned home to the stunning state of Utah. He felt a small pang of homesickness at the thought. Little Josh had been keen to grab his hand and pull him around the various rows of wines, explaining the different types of grapes and what wines they were best used for. He was obviously in love with—and proud of—the place and his knowledge.

That was what was keeping Carter awake. They were so at home there, loved it so much—how could he stand by and see them lose it? He fully admitted that logically, this shouldn't be his problem. He hadn't seen Katherine for years, he'd only met the boy and Julian today, but the passion that they had all displayed for their home and business had touched him deeply. Over dinner, he had questions about the business and learned that late August or early September usually marked the beginning of the harvesting process, with the white grapes for the fresh, clean white wines ripening first. Then there would be a flurry of activity as the whole range ripened within a few days of each other, from those first whites up to the full-bodied reds, and this would last probably until the end of October. It really was a time for all hands to be on deck, as it were, but Katherine didn't have the hands to carry out the work. The grapes would pass their best, rotting in the fields, and this would obviously have a negative effect for years to come, not only on her stock levels but also on the vines themselves. If she missed this harvest, the business really was sunk for good.

As a man with a good business head on his shoulders, he could see clearly what needed to be done short-term. The place needed an injection of cash immediately to hire the staff to get the harvest done and the grapes safely fermenting. If the guesthouse could be finished off in time for the end-of-harvest festivals and parties took place, so much the better. It would at least give the winery some hope of a future until a long-term plan could be put into place.

If only things were that simple! There were so many things that complicated this situation. The obvious was reconciling Katherine's wine business with his Mormon religion; then there were his own future plans for his inheritance. Added to that was Katherine's pride and the fact that they were friends, and he certainly could no longer ignore how much he wanted her to be part of his life. They hadn't spent that much time together since they'd met up again, but he'd spent nearly every free minute thinking about her. His growing attraction to her was worrying at best.

Of course, he'd always thought she was beautiful, but he'd appreciated that beauty aesthetically, as he would look at a beautiful painting or a stunning example of architecture—at least he'd thought he had. He'd never coveted her for his own or been jealous of Josh; he'd been glad of her friendship and appreciated her great company. If his feelings had run deeper then, he'd managed to block them out very successfully.

Carter glanced at his bedside clock and groaned. It was after 5 am, and although it was Sunday when so many of his friends got to sleep in, Sunday was not a lazy day for him. He had church, then various activities he was involved in with his church group afterwards, and he really needed to get some sleep. Trying to quiet all the thoughts whirling around in his head, he snuggled down and closed his eyes.

***

Arriving home on Sunday, Carter wasn't sure who to call first. He wanted to talk to Katherine and thank her again for yesterday, and he was anxious for an update on Carrie, but he didn't know whether to try the couple at home or leave them in peace and talk to Mom instead. He stared at the phone in his hand with a frown before finally making a decision and dialed the New York number before it got too late there. He was pleased when Antonio answered within the first two rings.

"Hi, it's Carter. How are you, and how is Carrie?"

"Hi, there! We're both as well as can be expected. She's home from the hospital but is being as stubborn as a mule. She wanted to go to church today, but the doctors have told her almost complete rest is essential. She's not confined to bed, but she's to take things very easy. She eventually gave in since it was far too soon for her to be going out. A couple of women from church paid her a visit instead and told her about the meetings and lessons; then they prayed together. But even that exhausted her. She's sleeping now."

Despite his reassurances, Carter could hear the worry and strain in his brother-in-law's voice. "Has she given up the ridiculous notion of continuing to work?"

A huge sigh from the other end gave him his answer before Antonio even spoke. "No, she's still insisting on it. I don't know what to do with her, Carter! She just won't listen. She is accepting that physically she must do everything to protect the babies, but she's not taking mental stress into the equation at all. She won't admit that her job is high-pressure and that being mentally fatigued can do as much harm as physical exertion."

"Maybe you should take her out of New York, away from the place she associates with work. You know the temptation to go into the office will be hard for her to resist."

"That might not be a bad idea if I can talk her into it. I already suggested going home to Utah; Grace has offered multiple times."

"What was Carrie's response?"

"She says that while she would love to have her family around her, they would fuss too much and make her feel like an invalid. She said it was far too early…wait a minute, what was the expression she used? Ah, yes, too early to have everyone clucking over her like mother hens. It would drive her crazy."

"Yeah, I get that." The shadow of an idea that had been floating around Carter's mind began to take shape and solidify. "Antonio, do you know anything about wine?"

"I'm Spanish—of course, I know about wine!" Antonio laughed. "Why do you ask?"

"Well, I have a friend who owns a vineyard, and she's shorthanded for the harvest. I want to do what I can, but you know how people are about accepting a helping hand. There is a beautiful guesthouse right there on the property. Maybe if you could convince Carrie you really want to visit California during harvest season, you could get her to take a vacation. I thought if you knew enough, you could lend a hand, and Carrie would be forced to relax and enjoy the scenery and the fresh air. You'd actually be doing me a huge favor."

"My family owns quite a few vineyards; I certainly know what needs to be done during harvest. Would I be able to tell Carrie that you really need me? It might convince her to go."

"Yes, but only if you swear her to secrecy. I'm going to play it the other way for my friend—that my sister really needs a quiet place to stay away from the smoggy city where she won't be tempted to work, and that she'd be doing me a favor by agreeing to have you. We're not actually lying to either of them, just being careful with how we play it for both their sakes."

"Hmmm…I think it could work, and it would be a huge relief to get Carrie away from here for a while. Perhaps an extended stay at this vineyard would enable her to feel she could cope with the family and we could head straight to Utah from there. Of course, we'd need the doctor's clearance for her to fly. Everything is stabilized, but we'd really need to check to be sure it's safe for all three of them."

"Of course you would. Before you go to that trouble, let me make another call and call you right back. I need to make sure I can get my friend on board."

Carter hung up and prepared to make his second pitch. After explaining the situation to Katherine, she answered immediately.

"Of course! I'd be happy to have your sister and her husband visit, but you know the guesthouse isn't ready. You saw it for yourself."

"Let me hire contractors to finish it, Katherine."

"I couldn't let you do that!"

"Please, for the sake of the babies. If it bothers you, you can pay me back when the business is thriving again."

He heard a sob at the other end. "That's never going to happen, so I'll never be able to pay you back."

"That doesn't matter. Katherine, please, thinking she's helping me out by coming will be the only way she'll agree. I don't want to lose my nephews or nieces before they even have a fighting chance."

He could almost hear Katherine pulling herself together at the other end. "Put like that, how can I refuse? Okay, we have a deal, but I will find a way to pay you back. My only worry is that I won't be able to hang on to the place long enough for them to see all the end-of-harvest festivities."

"We'll make sure of it somehow. I'll get on to the contractors first thing; with a bit of luck, they'll be on-site before the end of tomorrow. I can't thank you enough for this."

"I'm not sure who should be thanking who here, but never mind. Let me know when they're coming in, and I'll get them at the airport."

"Might not be necessary," Carter grinned. "If all goes according to plan with my boss tomorrow, I'll be staying too."

"I'm getting the feeling there's more to this than meets the eye, Carter, but I'll let it go for now. I'll hear from you again once you've finalized the arrangements?"

Carter was still grinning when he hung up. Step one of his plan was in operation, and it felt good. Josh and Katherine had worked hard on the guesthouse, and finishing it would take very little time and money. This side of the business was only property rental; he didn't have to sweat over the moral ethics for that. Those problems were still to come if he decided to follow through with the rest of the tentative—and some would say "half-baked"—plan that was still swirling around his head.

Chapter Seven

As the rising star of the company, Carter had no problem getting his boss to agree to an extended vacation at short notice. After all, he'd only taken some long weekends here and there since he'd started with the firm. He hadn't had any problems finding a local contractor to act as project manager for the completion of the remodeling in the guest house. They'd worked together before and enjoyed their joint projects. They agreed to begin immediately and outsource anything they couldn't handle.

Everything was working out, and all Carter was waiting, for now, was a call from Antonio to see if Carrie had taken the bait. The answer came in the form of an email saying that Carrie had agreed immediately to help out a friend of her brother's by lending her husband's expertise. They had a doctor's appointment the next day to double check that everything had settled enough for her to fly, and if the doctor agreed, they'd be on their way.

As Carter suspected, it wasn't long before he received a call on his cell phone. "Hi, Mom, how're things going?"

"Oh, fine, apart from hearing that Antonio and Carrie are about to go and work at a winery."

"Carrie won't be lifting a finger, Mom, I swear."

"I know. Antonio filled me in on your little plan. I'm not sure whether to be horrified you were so conniving or to thank you and call you a genius."

"You can do both."

"I could. Instead, I'll ask you a question. Do you think it's ethical to be involved in the production of alcoholic beverages?"

"I had this discussion with my friend, who's also in the church. She pointed out that there could be many less-than-ethical professions. It gave me a lot to think about and include in my prayers. All Carrie will be doing is resting and enjoying the fresh air and beautiful scenery. As for Antonio, well, I don't know. Katherine can't afford staff to get through the harvest, so in the end, he might be doing nothing other than taking care of Carrie. It depends on how things work out. At the moment, I'm leaning toward the decision that all we're doing is picking fruit. We're not involved with what happens to that fruit after that."

"That's a bit of misdirection, don't you think?"

"You mean a cop-out?" Carter laughed. "Well, maybe it is, but as I said, I'm praying about it, and it feels to me like helping a friend in need is more important than what happens to those grapes. As long as I'm not drinking the stuff, I don't think I feel compromised. Besides, these are high-quality wines being sold to restaurants all over the world or to dealers and collectors, not the stuff that ends up in bargain buckets in supermarkets or liquor stores. The people that appreciate this product are responsible drinkers who appreciate the artistry of the natural process."

"I'll need to give all that some thought and prayer myself before I come to a decision. Just remember that Antonio is still quite new to everything, and giving up wine must have been hard for him. Remember that he might struggle, and don't let him give in to temptation."

"I won't. I promise I'll take really good care of them both."

"I know you will, but if it all comes off, I might just take a small trip out there myself at some point just to see how Carrie's doing."

Hanging up the phone, Carter grinned. He'd been relying on Grace coming to that very conclusion. He was fairly certain that Maggie and Nigel would be invited along too, and once there, he had a feeling they would agree that saving a woman and small boy's beloved home was the biggest issue here and come to terms with the other matters within themselves. They were Christians, and as such, their values were to love and accept others, never judge, and help other people wherever possible. Everyone was going to love Katherine and Josh Jr. once they met them, and his family would rally to help in whatever way they could. He just knew it.

***

Over the next few days, Katherine grew more excited yet anxious at the same time. The work had been completed, and the guesthouse looked amazing. She knew that Carter's family was well-to-do and used to a high standard of living. She didn't want to be embarrassed by her scruffy, outdated houses. That was part of the reason she had agreed when Carter called and said that everything was set with Carrie and Antonio. They would be arriving shortly, but he had a sneaking suspicion that more of his family might want to pay a visit at some point, using the excuse of a vacation to check up on Carrie.

If she took a turn for the worse or was not granted permission to fly when her time grew near, he'd told her he had no doubt they would all arrive en masse with little warning and asked if she would be willing to rent out rooms in her own home. If they all came at once, they would need more than the eight bedrooms the guesthouse contained, so he wanted the contractors to begin on her house immediately. Wanting to provide them with the best she could offer, she had agreed, and the work was now well underway. At present, she was sitting in the tasting room with her laptop, trying to go over her accounts. The contractors were currently ripping out her ancient kitchen in preparation for the installation of a replacement, and Katherine couldn't hear herself think in the house with all the noise.

Frowning as she did the math, she looked at the figures with despair. Even if all sixteen bedrooms were rented out for a couple of weeks over the harvest period, it would hardly make a dent in what she owed. Besides, since Carter was paying for the renovations, she really wouldn't feel comfortable with his family paying rent, although he was insisting on it. No matter how she looked at things, she was finished. Even if she could convince the bank to extend the loans based on her two recently renovated houses available for vacation rentals, there was still the other problem to handle.

Thinking of the poor girl with those tiny, delicate lives inside her, she prayed that the meager amount she would be able to hand over would keep the lenders satisfied for a short while and leave her and Josh alone. If she could just hold things together long enough to help out Carrie and her husband, then at least having the winery would have done some good and served a worthwhile purpose. After that, she would have to think seriously about her very limited options. With nothing else to do, she closed her accounting program and began to plan out menus for her guests, making lists of groceries she would need. She would make the trip later, once she had plucked up the courage. All she could do was hope they would agree to the small sum buying her more time.

***

Carter was packed and ready to go. He was excited to take his first real vacation in several years, and that excitement was only intensified by the thought that he would be seeing Katherine every day. In order to give Carrie and Antonio privacy, it had been agreed that they would have the house to themselves for as long as possible, with Carter staying in Katherine's home. With a final check over his apartment, he picked up his bags and headed for his car. It had been delivered as promised, and he was looking forward to the drive to get to know the vehicle. After stowing his bags in the trunk, he climbed in, buckled up, and headed for Livermore Valley.

On the drive, he tried not to make too many plans, promising himself he would take things slow and see how things worked out, both from a business and personal point of view. He finally had to admit that he wanted to move heaven and earth for this woman—he would give her the stars if they were his to give. It was a disconcerting thought.

He was happy that he had finally found someone he could love with all his heart, but he had to wonder if he had always felt that way about her. Had he broken an unspoken code and been in love with his best friend's girl all these years? Was that why no one else had ever managed to measure up and capture his heart? Every moral fiber in his body argued against it, not wanting to think of himself in that way. But if he looked deep into his heart, he had to admit it was true, even though it was a truth he'd been blind to for all this time and would never have acted upon even if he'd known.

On top of the realization of this failing, he had to consider the fact that she wasn't as fully immersed in the faith as he was, even though it was still important to her. If he loved her, he would have to accept that fact about her, and that would mean they could never be married in a temple. *Stop it!* He chided himself. He hadn't even asked her on a proper date yet, and she had only recently lost her husband. He didn't want a relationship based on grief and loneliness; it had to be the real thing. If it couldn't be, he would rather settle for friendship. If a lifetime of unrequited love were his path to walk, then he would walk it without complaint.

The journey was over too quickly for Carter to form any more thoughts, and he was glad. One tiny baby step at a time was the best way forward. Pulling up outside the house,

Katherine appeared at the door to greet him, Josh hot on her heels.

"Carter, Carter!" yelled Josh. "Julian says the white grapes are telling him they'll be ready in a few days. Come and see if you can hear them whispering to you, too," encouraged young Josh with excitement bubbling over.

Josh grabbed Carter's hand, and all he could do was shrug helplessly with one shoulder and raised eyebrows as the little boy dragged him by the hand over to the shed where the four-wheelers were kept. Katherine's laughing face was the last thing Carter saw before he was plunged into the darkness of the shed. Flicking on the light, the boy made his way to a large door and opened it, hopping from foot to foot as he urged Carter to get the machine started.

Then easing the four-wheeler out of the shed, Carter waited while Josh closed the door behind them. Expecting Josh to hop on the back, Carter was surprised when Josh slid onto the four-wheeler in front of him, nestling himself up against his chest, tucking himself neatly into Carter's arms. With a pang, Carter realized this must have been something he did with his father while riding the vehicles necessary to traverse the full twenty acres of planted vines. Driving along with Josh pointing him in the right direction, Carter was hit by the mammoth task of caring for more than 10,000 vines for the first time. No wonder Katherine had said the vines were already beginning to suffer with only her and Julian to look after them. They were fighting a losing battle.

Spotting Julian, Carter pulled alongside, and the two climbed down. Josh immediately ran to Julian, asking what the grapes were saying today.

"Why don't you tell me what they're saying to you," Julian said.

The two men watched as the young boy tentatively approached the vine. He studied the bunches, then carefully reached out to caress the skin of a few select fruits. Finally choosing one, he softly pulled it from the bunch and popped it in his mouth. As he began to chew, he screwed up his face, causing the men to laugh.

"I think they're saying five or six days," he declared after swallowing the offending fruit. "Not sweet enough yet."

"Close," Julian said. "More like three or four. Remember, these fruits aren't for eating—we need the balance of sweetness and acidity to make a crisp white."

Josh nodded sagely, wise beyond his years. "Of course, I forgot that the first grapes make the young whites, which need to be crisp and fresh."

Carter listened intently as Josh continued to give him a lesson on the eight different wines the company produced and the optimum condition of the grapes for each one. He'd never drank wine himself, so he hadn't given this complex process a single thought in the past. It was a fascinating subject with so much to learn, but for such a tender age, Josh seemed to have grasped the basics with aplomb. *He must really love it here and love this life*, Carter thought as he listened to the boy give his simple explanations. Julian nodded confirmation in many places and gave gentle corrections in others, looking like a proud grandfather. Carter knew that there would be two very broken hearts if the bank foreclosed.

"So how many staff would you normally have over harvest?" he asked.

"We used to have ten full-time staff plus me, not including Joshua and Katherine. Ideally, we would want twenty at least for the harvest alone, not including the crushing. See that building over there? That holds bunks for up to forty workers. We're lucky that we're a full winery here and don't have to ship the grapes off to be crushed. Many migrant workers flock to the area during this time of year, so it's normally easy to get the extra staff you need well in advance."

"Aren't there machines that can help?"

Julian looked skeptical. "There are, but we've never done mechanical harvesting here. Not only is it rougher on the grapes, but the machine doesn't know which bunches to select and which to ignore. That can reduce the whole quality of the wine. Besides, each harvester needs a team of five, so it wouldn't help us much anyway."

"If there was a way to raise the funds, would the staff come back, do you think?"

Julian removed his hat and ran a hand across his brow before shaking his head. "They'll all have committed to other vineyards for the harvest by now. They would probably come back after that, but they won't let people down. Most of the experienced migrant workers will have been picked up by now too. It's all a bit late to go finding staff now."

"Does Katherine know as much about the grapes as you and Josh?"

"She does. When they first came, they were both very willing students, and they learned so much in that first year, before things, well…before they started having problems."

Carter was itching to ask more about the problems, but he was well aware of the young ears beside him listening intently to the conversation. "Okay then, if you had four knowledgeable overseers including Josh here, could it be done with inexperienced staff who'd never set foot on a vineyard before?"

Julian gave Carter's question some serious thought, and finally, he nodded. "I think it could be done if they could be found. Might be a bit of a shambles the first couple of days, but I guess if they're quick learners, they'll get into the swing of things." He looked quizzically at Carter. "Did you have something in mind?"

"I'm not sure yet, and I haven't run anything by Katherine. I'm just trying to get an idea of what it would take to get this done. One final question. If we could gather together the staff, are the grapes still good enough to produce decent wines?"

"This year, yes. If we'd lost the staff any earlier in the year, it would have been a different story, but we'd already done most of the cordon shoot removal, suckering, and leaf picking before we had to let them go. We've had perfect weather with no droughts and just the right amount of rain and sun to produce high yields of quality fruit. We've got enough to produce good quantities of very fine wines."

"Thanks, Julian. All that information is really helpful," Carter said. Although some of it went way over his head, he had the answer he needed. "Don't get your hopes up, but I'm hoping to find a way to get this year's harvest done and save the vines. It might not be a long-term plan, but it might help to bring the value of the place up to where it should be in a resale market."

"How about we meet up after dinner, and I can talk you through the cost per acre of harvest and crushing the grapes?"

"That sounds great! I'll look forward to that. Hey Josh, ready to head back to the house?"

"Sure, it's lunch time! Coming, Julian?"

"I'll follow along."

The three headed back to the house and were greeted by Katherine, who finally had a chance to say hello to Carter. She had collected his bags from his unlocked car and placed them in his room. The four of them enjoyed a pleasant lunch, with Josh chattering about how excited he was to be on holiday from school and begging Carter to take him to the fondue restaurant again. With a grin, Carter found it an easy promise to make.

After lunch, Katherine gave him a tour of the two houses, letting him see the excellent work that had been done. He was impressed with what the contractors had accomplished, but he was more impressed with the effort that Katherine had gone to when putting in the finishing touches in preparation for her guests' arrival tomorrow. The master bedroom was beautifully dressed with fresh linens, the en suite filled with fluffy white towels and toiletries. The house was peppered with an array of fresh flowers, giving the whole place a delicate perfume. The kitchen had been stocked with essentials, although Katherine said she would provide three meals every day if needed to save Carrie having to cook.

Outside, beautiful lawn furniture sat on a small patio, ideal for relaxing in the sun or under the shade of a huge umbrella. The place provided everything a luxury hotel would, with Carter's instructions to install air conditioning in every room, a high-speed Wi-Fi router, and even a hot tub outside by the patio. With the stunning views of mountain scenery, Carter couldn't think of a better place for Carrie to relax during her difficult pregnancy and hopefully get through it safely. He hoped that the mountain scenery would make her homesick and want to be back in Utah with her family for the final stages, but until then, she would want for nothing here.

He was pleased with how things had turned out, but he was slightly disconcerted with how little time he had to decide upon getting involved in the wine industry, even if it was on a temporary basis. Would he be compromising his beliefs? Would he be throwing good money after bad by investing in a struggling company? He realized he would have to make those decisions tonight; there was simply no more time to waste. If he had any chance of getting all hands-on board, he would need to act first thing in the morning.

Chapter Eight

Carter appeared bleary-eyed in the kitchen the next morning. The silence from outside compared to the constant buzz of the city he was used to having unnerved him, leaving him restless and sleepless. He'd stayed up late working at his laptop, inputting all the figures Julian had given him for how much stock the winery could expect to sell during the major tourist season of harvest time, along with the cost per acre for the harvest itself and readying the fruit for its long fermentation process. The figures weren't good, but with the newly upgraded rooms in both houses, perhaps he could ask Carrie and Antonio to move into Katherine's house, freeing up the guesthouse for full rental and bringing in extra income.

The problem was that the extra income needed to be applied to so many segments of the business, it just wouldn't stretch to them all. The cost of the harvest itself wasn't debilitating—not to Carter, at least—but he was aware that a vineyard needed a whole lot more than this once-a-year flurry of activity. The long-term forecast could be quite encouraging if Katherine would allow the injection of cash the place needed to get it back on its feet and to sustain itself.

What he couldn't factor in were the debts to be repaid. He knew he would have to be blunt and ask Katherine this morning. So much for tiny baby steps!

After praying intently, he'd come to the conclusion that morally, he'd already known that getting involved in the business was the right thing to do. Katherine had been placed back in his life for a reason, and he couldn't think of a better one than to help her save the home and business she and her son so obviously loved.

The fact that he had the means to do so when the timing was so drastic couldn't be a coincidence. He had to follow his heart and trust that God was the one influencing him to dive right in to a business he knew nothing about. It just felt like the path he was meant to follow, and if that was the case, then it couldn't compromise his beliefs. If he were wrong, then things wouldn't work out, and he wouldn't be able to pull it together, or Katherine would outright refuse his assistance. Carter had the faith that He would steer him safely through this confusing time. With laptop in hand, he prepared himself to broach the subject with Katherine.

After a hearty breakfast set by his smiling hostess, he opened his laptop and pulled up the spreadsheet he'd been working on, inviting her to sit beside him and see the tentative figures he had collated. He talked her through the projections, watching the smile fade from her face and getting tight-lipped as he spoke about the staff for the harvest.

"It really wouldn't cost that much. I've been talking to Julian, and with Antonio's help as an overseer, he thinks we could manage with untrained, inexperienced staff. He told me that we have accommodation already on-site so that wages would be less instead of board being provided. I was thinking of canvasing some of the local universities to try and get students to come and work over the summer holidays. I'm sure I could get more than interested enough; it would almost be more of an adventure for them than hard work. They get to spend the summer in the wine region, fully involved in the process, getting fed three times a day, be involved in all the parties at the end and go back to school with money in their pockets. I know it's short notice, but I'm sure we could do it. What do you think?"

"It doesn't matter how little it would cost, Carter, I don't have it."

Carter took a deep breath, knowing the dreaded moment was upon him. "I know you don't, but I do."

Katherine leapt from her seat, knocking it over in the process. "No, I can't let you do this. You don't want to get involved in this place, Carter—it's dragged us all down, and I don't want it dragging you down, too."

Carter stood and approached the pacing Katherine, placing a hand on her shoulder. "Please, calm down and listen. I've been working on all the figures. The money that this place needs to carry it for a year until after harvest is well within my means, and by then it would be self-sufficient again."

She whirled around to face him. "The last thing I need is more debt I have to struggle to pay back. Self-sufficient doesn't mean profitable enough to pay back everything I owe, and adding you to that picture wouldn't help."

"I never said anything about being paid back. Even if I did, I'm not a bank. I won't be looking for regular payments with accruing interest on the balance. You can pay me back in five years, ten, twenty, I don't care. This isn't about money; this is about you and Josh and your home."

Katherine dropped her head, breaking Carter's intense gaze. "Why?" she whispered. "What are Josh and I to you?"

Now it was Carter who turned away from her, unsure how to answer the question. He knew this would be a defining point in their relationship; everything this morning was make or break. He had to be truthful with her. "Honestly, I don't know yet. What I do know is that the thought of seeing both of you fills my life with joy, and spending time with you gives my life more meaning and purpose. I remember how close we used to be, the hours we spent talking. I want that again; I want to feel that connection. Where it might lead, I have no idea."

Carter turned back to face her, placing his hands on her arms. "I think I could fall in love with you, Kate, but I know it's too soon, and for now, I just want to be there for you, be a friend and see what happens."

Slowly, Katherine raised her head to look at him. A soft smile played across her lips. "No one's called me Kate in years."

"We always called you that. Didn't Joshua...."

Kate shook her head. "He stopped. Listen, Carter, I know you've got this image of me as the grieving widow, and I am sad that Joshua is gone—no one deserves to die that young—and the pain I feel for my son losing his father is indescribable, but if Joshua hadn't...." She choked on a small sob before composing herself. "Well...if he hadn't died, we would have ended up apart anyway. Our marriage was a disaster and went wrong within a few months of our wedding.

"I really thought that being a husband and father on top of a business owner would be the making of him, but it wasn't. He was just as irresponsible and reckless as he was when we were students. He never grew up, and all the love I felt for him slowly died as he let us down time and time again. We'd pretty much been living separate lives since our first wedding anniversary."

"Oh, Kate, I'm so sorry. I had no idea things were that bad."

Carter pulled her into a hug, holding her close while he digested this new information. He tried to quell the tiny part of him that was glad she hadn't still been as wildly and deeply in love with Joshua as she had been when he'd known the couple. It was selfish of him to think that way, even though Joshua's death would have hit her a lot harder if she had still been deeply in love with him. The thoughts weren't coming from consideration for Kate, they were coming from his own desire and hope of a relationship, and he knew it was wrong. He closed his eyes as he held her, silently praying for the strength to push the small spark of self-interest away and concentrate on what the woman in his arms needed right now: his comfort and sympathy. Kate pulled away from him.

"No one knew except Julian. He was so close to us that he couldn't help but notice, I guess. Then afterward, he was my only friend, and I desperately needed to talk to someone. We had kept everything hidden for so long for Josh's sake."

"I understand. I'm glad you had someone and didn't go through this completely alone. What about your family? Didn't anyone come to stay, to help you through it?"

"My family doesn't really talk to me much, not since the wedding. They didn't approve of Joshua and more or less said if I went through with it, they were done with me. I never bothered contacting them."

Carter couldn't imagine life without the support of his large family. He knew that even if he chose a partner who didn't share their faith or hold the same values, they wouldn't ever cut them, or him, out of their lives. He felt a sense of dismay that people could be that way. It certainly wasn't in their teachings, but he could understand that her parents would want the best for their daughter, and they were worried that Joshua wasn't it. Perhaps the threat had been an empty one, a false ultimatum to try to make her see sense—one they regretted to this day. Still, that was a problem he had no business in. Not at the moment, anyway.

"That must have been a tough choice to make."

"Not at the time, although I would give it more thought now; hindsight is a wonderful thing. I was so young, and Joshua was so exciting, so…free. You can imagine what it was like, coming from the strict rules of the church. Here was a guy who had no rules, who embraced every aspect of life and lived it to the fullest, never thinking of consequences." Kate lowered herself back into the kitchen chair she had absently righted. "There are times when I wonder if I was ever truly in love with him, or if I was just infatuated with his whole way of living, of being. There have even been times when I wondered if I chose the wrong roommate."

She glanced shyly at Carter and looked away quickly. Carter's heart pounded wildly in his chest as he wondered if he had heard her correctly. Judging by the attractive pink flush on her cheeks, his hearing was just fine. Warmth filled him, and joy lifted his soul. There was hope that maybe, just maybe, she and Josh could fall in love with him, too. He sat back down beside her and took her hand.

"So, we're agreed that there may be something here, but if not, we stay friends?"

Kate nodded, and Carter seized the moment. "So on that basis, shall we get back to business? If you'd let me help you, in the spirit of friendship and maybe more, we can do this. Together."

After all that had transpired, Carter was confused and dismayed when Kate burst into tears, hiding her head in her hands. Through her sobs, he barely managed to make out her words.

"There's so much more Carter, more than you know. Everything is such a mess, and it isn't safe here. I shouldn't have agreed to let your sister come. You should just go, pick them up from the airport and take them anywhere but here, as far away as possible."

Carter placed a comforting arm around her shoulders, letting her crying burn itself out yet again before speaking. "What on earth are you talking about? I won't let the banks foreclose, and no matter how bad the debt, I'll work some arrangement with them. I might only be an architect, but my father was a shrewd businessman, so I know my way around a negotiation."

"It's not the banks I'm afraid of, Carter. Oh Lord, things are so much worse than that. I don't even know how to tell you."

"Come on Kate, just spit it out. Whatever it is, we'll face it together."

"That's what I'm afraid of. You shouldn't get involved, but I know I won't be able to stop you."

"Involved in what?"

Even Carter was beginning to worry now. She sounded so afraid, so desperate. He couldn't even begin to imagine what trouble she could be in to cause a reaction like this. He anxiously watched as she took a deep breath, wiped her eyes, and reached for a tissue to blow her nose.

"I hadn't been involved in our finances at all. Joshua wanted to handle all that so, like an idiot, I let him, leaving it all to him. I had no idea we were so broke until I visited the lawyer in the city that day, just before running into you. Of course, when I got back, I went hunting through the financial records. I found several large withdrawals from our account— I mean *huge* withdrawals—and for the life of me, I couldn't understand what they could possibly be for. The last major outlay that wasn't a regular expense was the four-wheelers. Checking over the mortgage details, they certainly hadn't gone to reducing the loan. In fact, it's in arrears by quite a few months. I also found he had been neglecting to pay our creditors, so if he wasn't paying the mortgage or bills, where was the money going? It was a complete mystery to me until I got the first letter."

"Had he taken out another loan or a second mortgage?"

"Worse than that. Apparently, Josh had developed a taste for gambling, and his creditors want me to pay up. Soon."

Carter frowned. "Look, I'm not a lawyer, and although all the debt he ran up by not paying the bills has to be dealt with, I'm pretty sure you can't be held responsible for the personal debt that way. What did your lawyer say?"

"You're not getting it, Carter. This isn't a casino or something where we can pursue the debt through legal channels. I can only imagine they were some sort of back street, illegal games with no rules. They're not sending me polite debt collection agency letters, they're threatening me!"

Carter paled. "Threatening you? How?"

"First it was the vineyard, saying they'd burn the place to the ground, then it was me, physically. I can't even repeat what the letters said, but they're escalating, and now they're threatening to take Josh. I don't know what to do!"

Kate was hysterical, and Carter felt almost as helpless, having no experience with this type of thing or these types of people. "Have you spoken to the police?"

"I can't." Kate was pacing now, covering the length of her newly remodeled kitchen. "They said that if I talk to anyone, anyone at all, they'll kill me. What would happen to Josh if anything happens to me, Carter? I don't even have a family I can rely on to look after him; he doesn't even know his grandparents. He would probably end up in state custody. What about when he grows up, will they still be looking for the money? I can't see a way out of this; I can't afford to pay them off, and even if I could, would they leave me alone? What if they decide I'm an easy mark and just keep wanting more and more?"

Carter felt physically sick at the thought of Kate and Josh being dragged into this, at the thought of anyone laying a finger on her or her son. How could his friend have turned into such a selfish coward, leaving her here alone to deal with his problems?

He had to admit that at the moment, he was too blindsided to see a way out. Maybe Joshua thought taking his life would end the debt and the problem. Perhaps it was some grand gesture to try to save her. If it was, it hadn't worked. Carter was probably just as afraid for Kate's life as Joshua had been for his own, but he wasn't going to run. He wasn't going to abandon her.

"I don't know, Kate. I wish I did, but right now I can't think. I'll need some time to go through it all in my head, but I'm sure we'll think of something. How much did he owe?"

"Originally, it was just over eighty thousand dollars, but they're applying a ridiculous rate of interest, and it's now well over two hundred thousand. At least it was the last time they contacted me. It'll probably be more than that now."

Carter hid his shock at the amounts involved just for playing a game. This was serious money. "They haven't been in touch recently?"

"Not for a couple of weeks, although I have noticed a strange car hanging about. I'm so scared they're waiting for their chance to act on some of their threats."

Kate began to sob again, and Carter wrapped her in his arms. "Hey, come on. I might have no idea what to do right now, but I'm sure I'll come up with something. You have Julian and me here, and very soon Antonio and Carrie will be here, too. We can all help keep an eye on you both. We just need to stick together and work it through."

"That sounds like something you're used to."

"I guess it is. The family always rallies around if anyone has a problem. We've always been there for each other. I'm truly blessed by each one of them. The same holds true for the men my sisters have married."

"You really should change your mind about bringing your sister here. It could put her in danger, or if something were to happen, it might put the babies at risk."

Carter frowned. "I kind of wish I could, but even if I told Carrie what was going on, it would just make her more determined to be here and help. It's obvious you haven't met my sister! Besides, I'd feel better with more people around the place, and Antonio will be very useful to have around. Talking about having people around, are you up for getting through this harvest?"

"You still want to be my knight in shining armor?"

"I do, more than ever."

Kate managed a plucky smile. "Then I'm in."

"That's my girl! Let's get this started," Carter replied with a grin.

Chapter Nine

With Carrie sleeping soundly, Antonio and Carter sat out on the patio, making use of the brand new lawn furniture while Carter filled him in on the events of the last few weeks, right up until the point he had collected them from the airport earlier in the afternoon. In his usual manner, Antonio sat with a stoic expression, listening carefully to every word, but giving nothing away. When Carter explained the revelations from his talk with Kate in the morning, Antonio had glanced longingly at the tasting shed but had resisted temptation with a sigh and a shake of his head, turning his attention back to Carter's story.

"So that's where we're at. I've got eight students signed up already, arriving tomorrow, and I'm hoping that by tomorrow we'll have quite a few more. Some expressed an interest but not for the full three months, so I prepared a spreadsheet so we can fill in each week. I know it'll be harder having staff changes, but if it's what we have to do, then so be it."

"I'm quite certain we'll handle the harvest and have an excellent crop. That's not the part that's concerning me, Antonio responded.

101

"Right, sure. Look, I'll understand if you want to leave. This isn't what I had in mind when I asked you to come here. If I'd known, I never would have involved you guys. It would be for the best if you just went to Utah from here and took Carrie home."

"It would be, but you know it'll never happen. Even when I explain to her, she'll be determined to stay. She won't abandon you, and neither would I. We're brothers now, and brothers take care of each other."

Carter nodded. "I was afraid you'd say that. I've made a mess of things, jumping in with both muddy feet before all the full facts. If anything happens to any of the four of you, I'll never forgive myself."

Antonio chuckled. "You followed your heart, and we responded. Once we decide to stay, which I'm sure we will, then the responsibility is off your shoulders and firmly onto ours. If this is the path we must follow, then we accept it, so you have no need to worry, and forgiveness isn't necessary. If it is, you have to seek it from a higher power than ourselves."

"You're absolutely right, of course. Thanks for that, Antonio. I needed to hear it."

"So about our other little problem—have you given it any consideration?"

"I've tried," Carter sighed, "but I'm drawing a blank right now. I asked Kate if she could just hand the property back to the bank and run. I'd gladly take her back to Utah, but she thinks they'd just find her again. She doesn't want to be on the run, always looking over her shoulder for the rest of her life."

"Is there any chance these are empty threats designed to just frighten her into paying up?"

"I wondered that too, but she showed me the letters, and now I don't think so. I think they're absolutely serious, and if she doesn't pay, they won't let it go. They need to make an example of the situation to let others see there's no way out, not even death. Anything else would look weak, and they'd lose power."

"Money isn't exactly a problem for any of us. Why don't we just pay them?" Antonio questioned.

"Would you?"

"Absolutely not! I wouldn't give a penny to scum like them; it would be condoning everything they stood for and allowing them to treat others the same way. I wouldn't bring this on any other family. If the debt were mine, I would pay the sum I owed as a matter of honor but not the ridiculous interest. But they can't place the responsibility for one person's actions upon another this way."

"I feel the same. It isn't about the money, it's the principle involved, but you have to ask, are our principles worth dying for?"

They two men stared at each other, considering the question. Carter slowly began to nod.

"Principles, morals, ethics, beliefs, call them what you like. It's what we stand for and strive for. What good are they if you aren't willing to offer the ultimate sacrifice for them? If you back down at the first sign of trouble, they're worthless. My answer is yes, of course, they are."

"Good answer, brother," Antonio grinned. "So we don't run, we don't hide, we don't roll over and pay up—we find a way to fight and win!"

***

"Anderson, Anderson and Colby, how may I help you?"

Carter raised one eyebrow at the receptionist's words at the other end of the telephone but covered his surprise. "Peter Anderson, please."

"Whom shall I say is calling?"

"Carter Carpenter."

"One moment."

Carter heard a click and a few seconds of elevator music before the call was picked up again. "Carter, Peter here, good to hear from you. Everything all right with Carrie? Did she arrive safely?"

"Carrie's just fine; she's in the kitchen keeping Kate company while she prepares dinner, no doubt trying to wheedle her way into helping out."

Peter's laugh was warm at the other end. "No doubt. So what can I do for you?"

"I need to discuss something with you at length. Is this a good time?"

"Personal or professional?"

"Umm, both I guess, but it's your professional opinion I want. You see—"

"Stop right there. If this is a professional matter, don't say another word. Is your laptop handy?"

"Yes, why?"

"Log into your banking, and once you're in, I need you set up a transfer. I'll give you the details when you're ready."

Slightly bemused, Carter did as he was asked. He shrugged as he got the screen ready to put through a transfer. Everybody needed to make a living. "Okay, ready."

Peter gave him the bank details for the firm, and Carter typed them in and read them back to confirm. "Okay, so how much do you want me to send?"

"One dollar."

"What?"

"Send one dollar, confirm it's gone through, then hang up. I'll call you back when I see it on this end. Put my name in the details box. That's all, just my name."

Having no clue what was going on, Carter followed the instructions. It didn't take long for his cell phone to ring. He answered quickly, keen for enlightenment.

"Carter, I don't know what trouble you're in, but I recognize that tone of voice from past clients. Congratulations, you've just retained me as your lawyer to represent you in all legal matters, and everything you tell me is now absolutely confidential under the lawyer-client privilege. I can't disclose it to anyone, not even under police interview unless you give me permission to do so. It also means you have an official record of the conversation should you ever need it."

Carter was impressed—Peter knew his stuff. "Thanks for that. I have no idea where this might go, but everything you just said is good to know. By the way, did I hear right on the phone that the company name has changed?"

"Yep, it's not just Anderson and Colby anymore. Dad made me a partner in the firm just last week."

"That's terrific, Peter, I'm really pleased for you. You deserve it."

"Thanks, I hope I can live up to it. Now, what's going on?"

Peter's friendly manner was gone, and he was all business. Carter launched into the whole sorry story yet again. There was silence for a few seconds when he finished, then Peter's clipped tones kicked in. "It's personal debt, so legally they can't pursue it now that the debtor is no longer living. If we know their identity, we have a strong case against them, not only for trying to illegally pursue debt and for the illegal interest rates, but also for the threats, not to mention running an illegal gambling den in the first place. This isn't a reputable casino; they would have scrapped any marker they couldn't pursue through the courts. It might sound like a lot of money, but to a real casino, it's small potatoes and no great loss to them compared to what goes over those tables on a daily basis. Do you have anything to go on about their identities?"

"Not that I know of; none of the letters were signed. The only thing Kate has actually seen is a strange car hanging about the place."

"Any details on the car?"

"I didn't think to ask."

"Okay, see if you can find out anything at all. I would also suggest you hunt through the deceased's belongings, see if you can find anything relating to the place—a name, an address, what nights they operate, anything at all. Once you've done that, call me right back."

"I will. Thanks, Peter."

"No problem. And Carter?"

"Yes?"

"Stay safe."

"I'll try."

Carter hung up, feeling relieved that another almost-member of his extended family knew the situation and would offer any help he and his father could. There was no doubt that it was a relief to share the burden, despite the guilt for involving them. Having two capable men on his side almost made him optimistic that a solution would be found. He glanced at his watch, realizing that the minibus he had dispatched to collect the first load of students would be arriving soon. He hurried to the kitchen to see if there was anything he could do to help prepare for their arrival. He'd already helped Kate air out the bunk shed and make up the beds with fresh linens, but there would be a lot of mouths to feed in an hour or two. Thank goodness, he chose industrial-grade equipment for her new kitchen—they were going to need it! As he entered the room, Carrie was saying goodbye and hanging up her cell phone with a worried expression on her face. Carter placed a hand on her shoulder.

"Everything all right, Sis?"

"Umm, I'm not sure. I've got a confession to make."

Carter sat down across from her at the table where she was seated. "You told Mom, didn't you?"

"I couldn't help it," Carrie wailed. "You know she's got a freaky sixth sense if there is anything the matter with any of us. I tried to put her off the scent, but she badgered it out of me."

"I don't blame you," Carter said, shaking his head ruefully. "I've been avoiding calling her for that same reason. I'd have crumbled too. What did she say?"

"Oh fishcakes, I'm afraid to tell you. Please don't be mad at me."

"I won't, I promise."

Carrie looked guiltily at him across the table. "She's heading out on the next available flight, and of course, wherever Mom goes, Maggie goes, so no doubt Nigel will be with them too."

Carter held a hand out across the table for Carrie to take. "You know what, I was just telling Kate the other day what a blessing it has been all my life always to have my family to rally around when something was wrong, so I either have to be honored to be loved so much or eat my words."

"Then I guess you'd better choose the former," Carrie laughed.

"I just hope I'm not putting you all in danger."

"If anyone is in danger, then we put ourselves there by choice."

"Antonio said the same thing."

"That's my man; I knew I married him for a reason! Besides, the more of us are here, the more we can protect Kate and Josh, right?"

"Absolutely. Let's find the silver linings in this situation."

Carrie squeezed his hand, glad to see the happy-go-lucky brother she knew and loved reappear. "Mom's going to text me with her flight arrival details, but she says they're going to rent a car, so don't worry about picking them up. Kate, can I get rooms ready for them?"

"Definitely not! If Carter will take over here for a few moments, I'll do it. Where should we put them?"

"If you don't have any objections, how about here with us? Carrie and Antonio should have privacy to enjoy this vacation as much as possible."

"No problem, Carter; here, finish chopping these and stir this one every few minutes."

Carter saluted and took over with a grin, happy to be useful. He knew that Grace was going to give him heck when she arrived, but at the same time, he was glad she was coming. His mother was just so…capable. Her very presence would be a comfort to everyone, and little Josh was about to discover what it was like to have a grandmother figure in his life. Carter was sure he was going to love it.

Just as Kate arrived back in the kitchen to take over, the sound of an approaching vehicle alerted them to the first batch of students. Carter dashed off to take care of them, leaving the girls to it. He returned jubilantly.

"Great bunch, and more than I expected. There are eighteen of them, and more signed up to come over in the next few days. I really think this might just work. They'll be along for lunch as soon as they've settled into their bunks and explored a bit. Guess it's good I got the larger bus."

"Eighteen? You said eight this morning! I don't know if I made enough food!" Kate cried with dismay.

Carter and Carrie glanced at each other with a grin. "Err, Kate? I think you've prepared enough for a small army. Everything's going to be fine. Relax and enjoy the experience."

Kate stood with her hands on her hips, frowning at the various pots and the food she had prepared. Finally, she smiled gratefully. "You're right. Thanks, Carter, you always know just what to say. For the first time in a while, I think maybe things do have a chance of being fine after all."

Chapter Ten

Carrie was bored. She sat outside on the deck under the shade of an umbrella with a novel open in front of her, but she couldn't concentrate on it. After a fun-filled lunch with lively discussions from the students, everyone had headed off for their first instructions on harvesting grapes, and she had been left all alone. She wasn't used to this much downtime, and it was driving her crazy already. Antonio had even banned her from bringing her laptop, convinced she would log into the news site and continue to work from here. She had to admit he was right, she would. Still, without even that, she couldn't think what she was going to do for the next few months. Nobody would let her lift a finger to help out, and if everyone else was going to be completely wrapped up in the harvest, she would be left to try to amuse herself. When the large, black SUV pulled into the driveway, she almost cheered with delight when the driver came into view. As the car came to a halt and people began to clamber out, she almost flung herself into Grace Carpenter's arms, feeling like a small child again.

"Mom, I'm so glad you came!"

"Heavens above, Carrie, what's wrong?"

"Nothing, nothing at all. I'm just so happy to see you and have some company. You too, Maggie," Carrie added, releasing Grace and turning to hug their long-time friend and housekeeper. "Come and sit down and I'll get us something to drink."

"No, you will not, I will," said a figure appearing from the back seat of the car, yawning widely and scratching her head. Carrie stared in astonishment at her younger sister. As always, she was disheveled, her faded jeans had rips in the knees, and her battered Converse shoes were unlaced. Her wild mane of dirty blonde hair sprawled around her head and down her back, unhindered and free.

"Cassie! What are you doing here?"

"Well, thank you for that warm and generous welcome, Sis," Cassie muttered. "It's good to see you too."

Carrie laughed. "I'm sorry, I'm just surprised is all. I'm pleased to see you—more than pleased. In fact, I'm overjoyed that you're here!"

The sisters hugged, and Cassie smiled. "That's more like it. Now what about these drinks you promised us?"

"Oh, Kate brought over a huge jug of freshly made lemonade. It's in the fridge."

Cassie wandered off to retrieve it while the other women settled themselves at the outside table.

"No Nigel?" Carrie asked, surprised that Maggie's husband hadn't accompanied them.

Maggie grinned sheepishly. "Oh, he's here, but he decided our choice of rental car was too boring for him. He went off in search of something a little more…exciting. I'm sure he'll be here soon."

Carrie nodded and giggled. Nigel's love of cars was something he had shared with her father, John. The two of them had spent hours discussing the merits of muscle cars and foreign sports cars, and their mutual interest was responsible for the whole five garages back home filled with her father's collection—everything from Bentleys to Ferraris. Carter was the only one who had inherited the interest; the rest of them considered cars simply as vehicles to get them from point A to point B in comfort, and nothing more.

As Cassie returned and poured lemonade for them all, the conversation was dominated by Carrie's health. She tried desperately to reassure them all that she was fine and didn't need to be fussed over, and while she wanted to do everything in her power to protect the delicate lives growing inside her, she was frustrated with the inactivity forced upon her and the boredom it was creating. The women seemed to understand, and they all promised they would do everything in their power to help her pass the time pleasantly. The roar of an approaching engine caught their attention, and they watched with amusement as a sporty four-door entered the main gates and sped up the driveway. A satisfied Nigel exited the vehicle, making his way over to the table.

"What on earth is that?" Grace asked. "I expected you to turn up in a canary yellow Lamborghini or something similar."

Normally quiet around the family, Nigel was happy to talk when it came to cars. "Thought it would be prudent to have the back seat, or else I might have. This ladies, is a BMW Alpina B6 Grande Coupe, but don't be fooled by the fact it's a coupe. It has a powerful 540 horsepower turbo-charged V8 engine and can reach top speeds of nearly two hundred miles per hour, zero to sixty in 3.7 seconds."

"Wonderful," Maggie replied with a large dose of sarcasm. "Now we can tour the entire state in a few hours and see the sights in a blur as we speed past. What came over you?"

"Thought it would be a nice change from hauling a great big beast like that around," Nigel shrugged, indicating Grace's choice. "Besides, it might come in handy."

The women went silent, contemplating his words. They had been avoiding the subject of the trouble that surrounded the vineyard, but Nigel's comment, as much as the words he didn't say, was a stark reminder of what Carter had unwittingly become involved in. Maggie gave Nigel a terse nod of approval, letting him know that perhaps his thinking wasn't quite as off-base as they had originally thought.

"Exit strategy, good plan," Cassie acknowledged. "So, Carrie, is there anything else you can tell us about what's going on here?"

"Not really. I pretty much told Mom everything I know on the phone, and there doesn't seem to have been any developments since we got here."

Their conversation was interrupted by a flustered and flushed Kate heading in their direction. "I'm so sorry I wasn't here to greet you, I had no idea you would be arriving so soon. Please, let me introduce myself. I'm Kate Peterson. Welcome to my home."

Introductions were made all around, and after assuring Kate they were fine for refreshments, she insisted on taking their bags to their rooms. Nigel was adamant he had to help, too, and as they left, Grace raised an eyebrow at Carrie. "Quite stunningly beautiful, and she seems very pleasant. Is there any romance between them?"

"Well, there's certainly lots of sparks; you can almost feel the attraction between them. I think they care deeply for one another, but I don't think it's progressed beyond friendship yet, although I have high hopes."

"It's about time Carter found someone. I was beginning to think that he would never settle down. It must be hard on him watching you girls all find your happily-ever-afters and not experiencing it himself."

"Oh, come on, Mom, Carter's a notorious flirt! You have no idea how many girls he's had swooning over him over the years!"

"I'm probably more aware than any of you ever realized," Grace said. "Casual dating and fun flirting is one thing, and I'm quite sure that some of those girls maybe did fall in love and hope for a future, but he never led them on, and he's never given his heart to anyone. We know that's only passing the time until the real thing comes along."

"Maybe for us, but not for him. You know how much he used to scoff at all our childish dreams of prince charmings and knights in shining armor. He was the best brother a girl could wish for, but he was still a brother! He had no time for all our Disney fantasies, telling us the real world just wasn't like that."

"And yet here he is, putting his life on hold and moving heaven and earth to assist a damsel in distress," Grace smiled with self-satisfaction. "I think Carter has just learned that those things can exist after all. He may not have the armor as such, but he's certainly playing the role of a knight and coming to her rescue."

"You're right; I hadn't thought of it that way. I wonder if he realizes it; if not, some teasing might be in order. Nothing like revenge served cold with a side of teasing."

The women laughed. "Let's wait until the relationship is on firm footing first. We don't want to panic the poor boy!"

***

After a long, exhausting day learning all he could about grapes and the harvest, Carter greeted his family enthusiastically. Sitting at the large kitchen table awaiting the arrival of the students for the meal, he grinned cheekily at Cassie. "So, what made you finally emerge from your garret?"

Cassie feigned indignation as she answered the question. "For one, I wanted to see my sister, and two, did you think for a minute I would miss all this? So much inspiration for new books! Besides, I can write anywhere."

"That's news to us since you've been holed up in that attic room for years. You'd better be careful in the sunlight; it's been so long since you've seen it you might spontaneously combust or something."

"You're not funny, Carter."

"I thought it was quite witty. Seriously though, thank you all so much for coming. Kate and I are truly grateful for your help."

None of them missed how he put their names together in his statement, as if they were already a confirmed couple. Grace's small, serene smile spoke volumes. The boisterous arrival of the eighteen ravenous students and an overexcited young boy, however, put an end to the serious conversation for the time being. It was only when Josh had been put to bed and the students departed for the bunk house that Grace had a chance to address Kate.

"Tell me, my dear, do you think you could handle any more guests right now?"

"Well, we have eight bedrooms in each house. Six are occupied here and one in the guesthouse, so yes, there's plenty of room for more if Carrie and Antonio don't mind sharing. Did you have someone in mind?"

"I'm sure they won't mind sharing when they hear the news. Both Chelsea and Courtney have expressed an interest in coming along, and of course, Kade and Peter would come with them. Do you think you could handle another four guests and three rooms? Obviously, we could do our own catering and help out with the laundry and chores and things."

"Oh, another four is no problem. I love to cook, and I'm cooking for so many anyway that another four is nothing. I don't know if we'd fit even one more around this table though. As big as it is, we were crammed together like sardines in a can tonight. We'd maybe have to stagger the meals and feed the students separately. How many did you say were coming tomorrow, Carter?"

"Another twelve have signed up, but after what happened today, I have no idea how many might actually show up."

"How about we set up trestle tables outside and put them together as one long table? That would be fun. It's more than warm enough, even after sunset, and it would save having to prepare separate meals," Cassie suggested.

"That sounds great! What do you think, Kate?" Carter asked.

"It does sound easier and much more sociable."

"Great, I'll get it organized. There's just one problem, though. We're going to need you on-site to supervise a crew, Kate. You won't have time to do the catering and stuff."

"That settles it then," Grace declared firmly. "Maggie and I will take over the running of the houses. Carrie, you can help with lighter jobs. You can be our official peeler and chopper sitting at the table here. Cassie, you'll help with heavier chores like laundry. The men can help you out, and the other girls will apply themselves to wherever they're needed most."

Both the girls agreed without hesitation. Carrie was delighted to be included and actually be of some use, and Cassie was keen to help. She knew she treated the main house back home a little unfairly, living in the guesthouse, completely absorbed in her writing and barely visiting even though it was practically a few steps away. This would give her a much-needed break and a chance to spend some quality time with her family, no matter what they were doing.

Kate, however, wasn't quite so convinced. "It's hardly a vacation if you end up having to do your own cooking and cleaning; that's really not acceptable."

"We're not here for a vacation; we're here to be of whatever assistance we can to Carrie and you and Carter," Grace clarified.

"I wouldn't argue with a Carpenter female, Kate," Carter laughed. "Once their minds are made up, there's no changing it, so you might as well just give in gracefully. Besides, it does solve a lot of problems that I hadn't really thought through enough Thanks, Mom. Are you serious about the others wanting to come?"

"Of course. They wouldn't see you in trouble and not be here to help."

"But how did they know? I spoke to Peter, but he wouldn't have said anything."

"I'm afraid I'm the guilty one there," Carrie admitted. "I've been so bored I've had nothing else to do except chat on the phone. What about the company, Mom? Can you spare them all at once as well as yourself?"

"Carpenter Global Press will run just fine without any Carpenters for a while. Charles will step in for me, and there are plenty of senior editors to cover Chelsea and Courtney's departments. We have a huge marketing team, and they'll just have to manage without Kade's expert direction for a while. Besides, we're all on the end of a phone and a short flight away if there are any problems."

Carter shook his head in disbelief; his mother's pragmatic approach to any issues never ceased to amaze him, and his family's willingness to drop everything and run to his aid was astonishing. He could tell from the shock on her face that Kate was also dumbfounded. Who knew that his actions would lead to a gathering of the entire Carpenter clan!

Chapter Eleven

With Josh and the students settled for the night and the new arrivals nestled in, it was finally time to address the problem Kate faced. The entire family was seated in the large living room, serious expressions on their faces. For everyone's benefit, Kate had stumbled through an explanation of events, bringing everyone up to date. She had produced the threatening letters, which each had read and passed along to the next. Right now, they were in Cassie's hands as she frowned at them, deep in thought, the last one to see them.

"These are terrible," she muttered.

"I know. It's a horrible situation that Kate doesn't deserve," Carter agreed.

"Well, that too, but that's not what I meant. I mean the letters themselves. Look at the grammar, the spelling, and the punctuation. It's awful! A kid on their first day of kindergarten could do better."

Courtney folded her arms. "I know you're a writer, Cassie, but is that really relevant? They're not going to be published."

Cassie leapt to her feet and began pacing in front of the assembled group, taking center stage. "It *is* relevant. This tells me that these men are not business people—they're unintelligent or uneducated goons, nothing more than hired brawn, and that indicates that they don't own whatever establishment Joshua frequented."

"They hold his marker, though. That's the point," Peter added.

"Yes and no. Look, I've done extensive research into criminal gangs across the states over the last few years and—"

"I thought you were a romance writer."

Cassie glared at Courtney's second interruption and folded her arms across her chest. "I am, but that doesn't mean I can't be anything else. I've been playing around with branching out for quite some time with my new partner," she grinned over at Antonio, who mock bowed in response. "We decided that some of my tentative plot lines could really come to life and be pretty juicy. Happy?"

Courtney nodded, satisfied with the answer, and motioned for Cassie to continue while the others looked on with interest.

"Before I continue, can I confirm that we're the only ones that know about this situation at the moment?"

"Julian knows some of it. He knows I'm being hounded for Joshua's gambling debts, but he doesn't know that little Josh has been threatened. He might suspect, though."

"But he's totally loyal to you and this vineyard?"

Kate nodded, while Courtney looked guilty. "Well...I had to tell Zac. When I told him I was going out of state, he obviously asked some questions. When I explained about the vineyard and the harvest, he thought it would be a great experience for the girls and was talking about coming down for a couple of weeks for summer vacation. I tried to put him off gently, but I just hurt his feelings, so I ended up telling him the truth. I didn't want the girls here because I didn't know how serious the situation was. I'm sorry."

"You made the right call," Carter said gently. Courtney's fledgling relationship with her real father was too new and delicate to handle deceptions, even ones by omission. He absolutely understood why Courtney had to tell him the truth and why she didn't want her little half-sisters anywhere near the place. "What did he say?"

"He just said to stay safe, keep in touch, and if he could be of assistance to let him know. He advised us to tread carefully, but he seemed to understand why we would all rush out here. He wasn't thrilled that I was about to get mixed up in it, but he understood that we would want to help a friend of the family. He won't tell anyone else, and whatever we decide to do, I'm sure he can be trusted with the information."

"Good enough for me," Courtney continued. "So, where was I? Oh yes, so when we think of crime bosses, we tend to think of the mob, the old mafia based in places like New Jersey, New York, and Boston, going back to the days of Capone, spats, and violin cases, right? The truth is, it still exists, and it's everywhere. Criminal gangs are as prevalent on the west coast as the east; they infiltrate every major city in the US, and nowadays, it isn't just the old Italian families, we have the Russians, the Columbians, the Chinese, the Irish, and the Estonians, too, to name just a few. It could just be speculation, but looking at the letters, the methods, the conduct of these people, I believe that this club, or whatever, is just a tiny part of a huge empire managed on a day-to-day—or night-to-night—basis by some pretty lowly members of a crew. They're probably supervised by someone who knows what they're doing, but I bet they've never even met their actual boss."

Carter noticed how pale Kate had become at Cassie's words. "Cassie, you're thinking like a writer. Don't you think that's maybe going a bit too far? You're probably letting your imagination run away with you."

"I'm thinking like a writer because I *am* a writer, and maybe I am getting carried away, but if I'm right, it could be to our advantage."

"How could it possibly be any better that Joshua owed this money to some mob boss and that's who's now after Kate?"

"Excuse me, but before you two start a full-blown argument, may I ask if anyone has ever considered just paying off the marker? I don't mean to sound pompous or elitist, but we're not exactly short of cash between us."

Carter's rising passion to protect faded at Courtney's words. The last thing he wanted to do was fight with his sister, especially when they were all here to help in any way they could. "We did discuss it, Courtney, but decided against it. Handing over that amount of cash would be like declaring an open day at the bank vaults. They'd probably see us as easy targets and come back for more whenever they liked. Besides, paying their usurious and illegal interest rates is out of the question. On principle, we decided no way."

"Fair enough, and for the record, I agree. I also think Cassie's speculation makes perfect sense. It's rare that these places are a one-off—they're usually owned by people who have legitimate businesses where they can hide the illegal earnings. What do you think, Peter?" Courtney asked.

"Yes, I agree with the girls, I'm afraid. Money laundering is a risky business if you can't do it in-house. These guys don't seem smart enough to run this operation undetected for any length of time. I definitely think they're just the hired help. When idiots like this are in charge, the smarter ones must be busy elsewhere. Although I don't know if I'd go so far as to mention a mafia, I think it's definitely part of a large syndicate of some sort."

Carter squeezed Kate's hand, attempting to reassure her in light of this devastating revelation. "I still don't see how this could be to our benefit."

"I was getting to that if I hadn't been interrupted," Cassie retorted. "If these guys have a boss, it means there's something they're afraid of, and we could use that to our advantage."

"Us?" Grace questioned. "How could we achieve that? I don't think any of us are familiar with this world or know how to operate in it."

Cassie grinned. "I think you're underestimating what we have here, Mom. What do you see when you look around the room?"

"A nice, wholesome, successful family of Mormons."

Cassie grinned. "Sure, but I see a whole lot more than that." Working her way around the room, she started explaining. "First, Antonio. A former heir to the throne, trained from the day he was born for the position. Not just a figurehead either—the future king of a country where the royal family are the leaders, the head politicians. He's not only a skilled negotiator but also an excellent judge of character. Those psychological skills are invaluable.

Next, we have Carrie, the head journalist of a prominent New York newspaper, one whose humanitarian approach to her job has earned her the love of people from all over the world. The website has a global following after the Spanish incident, not to mention the extremely public love affair. One phone call to her editor and we could have a front-page story about these guys and boy, wouldn't that make their boss edgy!"

Carrie grinned at her sister and shifted excitedly in her seat. She was starting to see where Cassie might be going with this, and it sure beats the boredom of sitting around doing nothing. Anxiously, she urged her to continue.

"Next, Kade and Chelsea. Chelsea, you've read so many plot lines you must have every possible scenario lodged in that brain of yours. You're a chief editor, skilled at looking for the tiniest plot hole or continuity error and making the corrections required to negate them. Whatever we come up with, you can pick it apart until it's watertight and flawless.

Kade, our marketing genius, can sell any story to anybody. He knows the exact wording, tone, and approach to pitching whatever we come up with to our goons and make them believe it without a shadow of a doubt. With the two of them on it, we can't fail."

Seeing she was starting to get the interest of the gathered group, Cassie carried on with a flourish. "Next we have Peter, not only a lawyer in a top law firm but a partner in that firm. He can guide us through this sticky situation, help out with contacts, and make sure that we don't actually do something outright illegal. He can also guide us in the workings of the criminal mind. Courtney, well, she could just as easily provide the same role as Chelsea and help, but she's also something more. She's daring and fearless, willing to take risks. In short, she's our wildcard. She's reckless and unpredictable and more often than not, it's those characters that save the day."

"You mean like Howling Mad Murdoch in the A Team?" Carter grinned, thinking back to one of his favorite old TV shows he used to watch as a child.

"Thanks for the comparison, guys!" Courtney huffed, folding her arms. "But I guess I can't argue with the point. If there were a way that involved risk, I'd likely be the one to suggest it and take it, too."

Cassie nodded. "Mom, Maggie, Nigel, you all provide wisdom and experience, the calm level-headedness that will keep us in check and stop us from getting totally carried away, reminding us that this isn't a game. And Nigel, you never know when your other little talent might come into play." Cassie winked at Nigel, who smiled in return, obviously acknowledging a secret shared between the two. "So all in all, we have an incredible team, and if we don't have the brains to outwit some bunch of goons, then who does?"

The gathering looked around at each other, seeing what Cassie saw for the first time. Some were smiling; some were nodding, agreeing silently with each of her assessments. The mood in the room had lifted slightly as if they had hope for the first time.

"So what's the plan, Cassie?"

"I don't have it all worked out yet, Carrie, but the basic premise is based on stereotypes. What do guys this low down in crews usually do?"

"Based on the movies and books, they usually take liberties when left to their own devices. Overstep the boundaries given to them, skim off the top, cheat the boss somehow," Carter replied.

"Exactly! So what if they were presented with hard evidence of this? What would they do if they were told this evidence would be presented to their boss within forty-eight hours if they didn't hand over the marker? And if they do, they have four days before we hand it over and run a headline story linking their boss to all his illegitimate businesses as well as the supposedly reputable ones?"

"They'd hand over the marker, then run for their lives and disappear off the face of the earth before the boss got to them," Courtney said.

Kate had been silent for the full exchange, but now she felt she had to intervene. "Cassie, this all sounds brilliant in theory, but it also sounds dangerous, and I'm not sure if I can let you get involved this deeply. Besides, we don't even know where this place is, let alone who the guys are or who they work for. How are we supposed to get this evidence?"

"We'll worry about the danger levels once we have a full plan in place. As for the evidence, if we can't get it, we make assumptions, fabricate it, and call their bluff. If it looks convincing enough, it won't matter if it's real or not. If they think the boss will believe it, it'll work. Anyway, we cross that bridge when we come to it. I think our first step should be to hire a private detective. We give him anything we can from Joshua's possessions and as much detail as we can about the car that has been hanging around. What can you tell us, Kate?"

139

"Not a lot, I'm afraid. The car was medium sized, silver, nothing special. As for Josh's things, well, I haven't even looked at them. I couldn't bring myself to go near them."

"That's worrying," Carter said. "Using a nondescript car, especially in such a bland color, suggests they may have more brains than we originally thought. Blends right in, and silver kind of disguises the make and model more than a vibrant color—less noticeable and easily forgettable."

"You're right," Cassie replied. "But let's not give up before we've even started. If it's alright with you, Kate, I'll forego grape duty tomorrow and start going through Joshua's things to see if I can get any clues. Carrie, if Grace and Maggie can spare you, you can help. Peter, can you recommend a good private detective?"

"Not in this area, but they're a close network. I'll make some calls in the morning to our regular guys and see if they know of anyone out here they could recommend."

"Perfect. So until we get the ball rolling, I suggest we all start thinking about a proper plan, but mostly, concentrate on this harvest and get this done. As long as we keep a close eye on Kate and Josh, I don't think there's immediate danger. Too many people around."

Kate gave a thankful smile to Carter, knowing that if it hadn't been for him, there would only be the three of them on this massive property, isolated and vulnerable. She had known the situation was serious, but she hadn't considered just how serious it could be. If these men were acting under the instructions of their boss to recover the debt, she and her son were in serious danger—far more than she had ever imagined. She shivered at the thought. Noticing how pinched and pale her hostess' face was, Grace stood up.

"Well, I think we all head to bed and get a good night's sleep. Things always seem clearer in the light of day. I have to admit, I was still torn over the moral connotations of helping out a winery, and now we're talking about scamming mobsters and possibly putting lives in danger!"

"Don't worry, Mom; we'll refine the plan so it doesn't go that far. It'll work out, and between us all, we'll find a way to make it something we can live with. You're right though, let's all head to bed. Busy day tomorrow."

With that, the group dispersed, each to toss and turn through the night with their own restless thoughts.

Chapter Twelve

The next morning, most of the able hands were out in the fields as dawn broke, ready for the next lesson in harvesting. The white grapes for the young, crisp white wines were almost ready. Any day now, the harvest would begin in earnest. They were only awaiting Julian's word to let them know that the grapes were perfect. Cassie, Grace, and Maggie had been up long before dawn, preparing a hearty breakfast for all. They had left Carrie to sleep, worried that the discussions of last night might have stressed her and raised her blood pressure, affecting the babies. They were busy clearing up when she emerged, tousled and ravenous, none the worse for yesterday's events.

"Any food left over? I'm starving!"

"We kept some back for you," Grace replied, slipping the plate that had been kept warm in the oven in front of her. "It's good to see your appetite's back."

"I think I've finally gotten over the morning sickness stage, although shouldn't it have stopped at three months, not coming up on five?"

"Usually yes, but with your blood pressure and everything, I guess that contributed. Also, your body is trying to get used to all the new medication the doctors put you on. Are you feeling okay?"

"I feel good today, Mom. The best I've felt in a long time. Oh, these eggs are delicious!" she exclaimed, cramming in another forkful. Grace smiled, happy to see her daughter looking and feeling more positive. Maybe the fresh air and these beautiful valleys were doing her good already. "Well, you are eating for three, so if you want seconds or thirds, just let me know," she joked.

Carrie nodded in all seriousness, her mouth too full to answer. Pushing her plate away after a hearty second helping, she leaned back in the chair contentedly, rubbing her tummy. "Thank you, babies, for letting me eat for a change," she said. "I'm sure we'll all feel better for it."

"Have you given any thought to names yet?" Grace asked.

"No, with everything that seemed to be wrong, we thought it best not to. Once everything has settled down though, I'm sure we will. I have a feeling that we're going to argue a bit over that. Lots of family members we'd both like to name our children after!"

"I'm sure you'll come to an agreement over it," Grace smiled, glad that her daughter now seemed much cheerier and more positive about the pregnancy.

Throwing the used tea towel into the laundry hamper, Cassie turned to Carrie. "Now that you've stuffed your face, are you ready to waddle on up to start going through Joshua's things?"

"Hey, I'm not that big," Carrie protested, rubbing the baby bump under her loose shirt.

"You will be if you keep eating like that, and it won't be the babies! Come on, Sis, Kate gave us permission to start in the bedroom. Apparently, she hasn't touched a single thing of her husband's, just left it all where it was. I'm quite hopeful that we'll find something somewhere in the house."

"What exactly are we looking for?" Carrie asked as they entered the master suite.

"I'm not sure, really, but I'm sure we'll know it when we find it. I guess anything that might give the private detective something to go on. The first place to always check: under the bed and under the mattress."

Cassie made her way over to the large bed, dropping to her knees to peer underneath. "Huh, nothing, not even dust," she said, disappointed.

"Would have been too good to be true if we'd found something in the very first place we looked."

"True. Why don't you take that chair over there and start going through the drawers of the tallboy, then the dresser? I'll try to lift this mattress and look underneath."

An hour later, they had been through most of the furniture in the room. The two had found lots of things that gave some insight into Joshua as a man, but nothing to give any firm clues to where or how often he gambled. They had found some promotional matchbooks in his nightstand drawer, and Cassie had put those in a pile on the bed, intending to check out the establishments online later. They had also found quite a distinctive lighter shaped like a tiny golden gun. It could give the investigator something to follow—people might remember seeing it.

"That leaves the closet," Carrie said, staring at the section of the room that was behind triple sliding doors.

"Don't tell me you're bored of this already? After all, it was all your idea."

"I'm not bored; it's just…well, it feels so wrong, hunting through a dead person's things like this. Also, it feels like we're invading Kate's privacy too."

"I know. I feel the same way. To be honest, it's giving me goosebumps, but we have to remember why we're doing it. We're trying to help, and if this is what it might take to protect them, then we have to get on with it."

"You're right. Pull the chair up to the bed, and I'll start bringing clothes over. You can check through the pockets, just in case. We'll start with jackets."

Once the wardrobe was empty of all Joshua's clothing and Carrie was meticulously checking each pocket, Cassie began rooting through the boxes on the floor of the closet. Most of them contained exactly what she expected: Kate's shoes. Then, tucked right at the back, she struck gold. The box contained a mish mash of items, several photographs of Kate and Joshua together, and others with little Josh also in the picture. They seemed to cover a long time span—select moments picked out from their lives together, frozen in time in glossy print. Putting the photographs aside for the moment, Cassie pulled out a thick envelope. Removing the sheets of paper, she found bank statements dating back for just over a year. The account was in one name only, Joshua's. The first balance on the statement was incredibly healthy, but regular withdrawals of $2000 had been made on a weekly basis, the sum dwindling until the final withdrawal all but emptied the account, leaving only a few dollars.

"Hey Carrie, take a look at this," Cassie said, rising from her cross-legged position on the floor to take the pages over to her sister. Carrie perused the pages, quickly taking in the details. "What do you make of it?" Cassie asked her.

"Keeping in mind your previous theories, I would speculate that perhaps he started gambling at a regular casino; I'm sure one of the matchbooks comes from a big one in San Francisco. Don't ask me how I know; it just seems to ring a bell. I think it might be a chain, and I've come across it somewhere. So maybe he hit it big one night—enough to attract the attention of people who run no-limits games.

Invited to join, he couldn't resist, so he opened the account to stash his gambling money away, hiding it from his family. Only judging by the finances of the business and personal accounts according to Carter, this wasn't enough to keep up with his losing streaks."

"I agree that's a really plausible scenario. It fits because almost every gambler thinks they're a good gambler, and if he hit it big once, he would be certain he could replicate it. They never think they're going to get into trouble. Losses are always temporary. If we're right, then it really gives the P.I. A great starting point to follow his trail. Any luck in the pockets?"

"Nothing so far. From what I can tell, everything has been laundered before being hung up."

"Okay, keep looking. I'm going back to that box."

Cassie once again sat down beside the box of treasure, sifting through what looked like mementos from a past life— ticket stubs, sea shells, and other trinkets that had been gathered during happier times. She finally came across a very small, tattered notebook, its thick card cover ragged and worn, bent in places and peeling apart in others. An elastic cord held the book closed and another attached a slim, black pencil with a gold-painted top. Slowly and carefully, she removed the band, opened the book to reveal the thin, lined pages inside. Each one was filled with a string of incomprehensible numbers and letters. She knew she was on to something big, but she couldn't decipher it. She was so excited that the numbers swam in front of her eyes and refused to make sense. She put it aside for further inspection. A final rummage in the box revealed nothing more of interest, so she replaced everything she didn't need. After tidying away everything she had dragged out, she began hanging up the clothes Carrie had gone through, careful to put them back just as she'd found them. On the second to last item of clothing in the pile, Carrie's fingers touched something slender. She pulled it free to find a business card with nothing but a gold, embossed symbol on one side. There was no name, no contact number, no company details, just an emblem made up of a poker chip and a dollar sign entwined. Flipping the card over, she saw a scrawled address on the reverse side.

"I think we may have got it!" Carrie declared excitedly, waving the card at Cassie.

Cassie looked at the card and grinned at her sister. "I don't know about a P.I.; we've found so many leads we could follow this up ourselves! We need to gather this stuff and show it to Kate and Carter."

They had just finished tidying the room and making their way back downstairs to dump their haul on the coffee table when the unmistakable growl of a Harley's engine penetrated the peacefulness of the morning. They glanced at each other, unsure if they should be afraid or not. Carrie whipped out her cell phone, ready to make the call that would bring the men rushing from the vineyard to their aid. From the window, they watched the four-wheeler meander its way up to the houses and pull to a stop outside, the helmeted figure sitting there perusing the property, allowing the engine to purr idly. Cassie made her way to the door, Carrie close on her heels. They opened the door and stepped outside, closing it behind them. Cassie stood in front of Carrie, shielding her with her body. Carrie kept her finger on the button that would call Antonio, holding off, not wanting to cause a panic if it was a false alarm.

They watched as the figure turned off the engine and kicked down the stand of the four-wheeler, easily swinging one leg over to get off. The torso-hugging black t-shirt and slim cut jeans over impossibly long legs that ended in scuffed cowboy boots told them the figure was all male, and powerfully so. Their nervousness increased as he slowly removed his tinted helmet, revealing long, dark hair and intense obsidian eyes. Cassie stepped back involuntarily as the figure took a step toward them, bumping into Carrie and causing her to drop the phone she had clutched in her hand. The stranger smiled a slow, easy smile, then spoke in a soft southern drawl.

"Nice to see I still have the same effect on the ladies. Jefferson Lakeland, private detective, at your service."

Cassie almost swooned with light-headed relief as the man held out his hand to shake.

***

Carter took the call then walked over to Kate, whispering in her ear. "P.I.'s here, we have to head up to the house."

Kate followed him away from the group and over to one of the four-wheelers that had been used to ferry the group into the center of the vines. More students had arrived early that morning, and they now had more than a full crew, albeit inexperienced. They wouldn't be missed for a while. Carter climbed aboard the vehicle, enjoying the warmth and the contact as Kate climbed on behind him, wrapping her arms around his waist. He took a deep breath, enjoying the scent of the valley as well as Kate's now familiar aroma, which reminded him of jasmine and vanilla. He started up the engine, and she squeezed a little tighter, causing Carter to revel in the closeness. There was no doubt he had fallen for her, but he was still surprised with the speed at which it had happened. He guessed it was similar to his sister's situation, where a week of almost twenty-four-hour-a-day contact and the intense situation, then the sudden separation from each other, had accelerated the process of falling in love for Carrie and Antonio. Knowing that Kate and Josh were in danger had intensified his feelings and forced him to acknowledge them, both to himself and to Kate. He had no doubt he would have fallen in love regardless, and the speed at which it had happened made it no less real, only more urgent. He was pulled from his thoughts by the sound of another four-wheeler following. A quick glance behind him confirmed that Peter had seen their departure and guessed the reason or had a similar call.

Pulling up to the house, Carter couldn't help but take a second or two to admire the Harley parked there. "Some machine," he said as Peter joined him.

"I don't really know much about motorcycles, so I really couldn't say," Peter replied.

"If it has wheels, it's my thing," Carter replied. "And I would love to get my hands on this for a test drive."

"Don't we have an appointment to keep?" Kate called, shaking her head at the two men as they stared at the four-wheeler.

Carter reluctantly moved away, admitting there were more pressing matters to attend to than his love of fast machines. Entering the house, they found all the women gathered with their guest in the family room. Introductions were made all around, and the newcomers took a seat while Cassie brought them up to speed, advising Kate that she might find some of the information hard to deal with.

Kate kept her face stoic throughout the reveal of what had been found, making no comment as she flicked through the bank statements before throwing them back onto the coffee table in disgust. Jefferson had kept his attention on the little notebook throughout, trying to decipher its meaning. With the others filled in, they all looked at him expectantly. Feeling their stares, he glanced up.

"Looks like this is all in some sort of code. I'm pretty sure some are dates, and others are sums; could be loses, wins, or withdrawals, maybe even some sort of gambling system. I'll figure it out, but I need to take some time cross-referencing it against the bank statements. The girls here thought he wasn't just using these funds, is that correct?"

"I believe so," Kate replied. "I found several frequent withdrawals from both our business and personal accounts that I can't reconcile, many of them pretty large amounts."

"Might help me to figure this out if I could have those too. Would help me establish any patterns."

"Can't we just go straight to the address we found?" Cassie asked, impatient to get past the preliminaries and into the most thrilling part of her rough plan.

"No, we'd never get past the front door. These games are invitation-only, strictly by appointment, and carefully guarded.

You can't just turn up. However, I can use the address to make some inquiries, see if any of my contacts know who runs the operation there. You've given me a few good leads to follow. Give me a few days, and I'll see what I can come up with."

After receiving the requested bank statements, Jefferson rose to leave, Peter escorting him to the door, where an intense discussion took place out of earshot of the others. Cassie watched Jefferson leave wistfully. "Shame he didn't stay longer," she muttered.

"Were you enjoying the view, dear?" Grace asked innocently but with a sly wink at Carrie. Cassie whirled round from the window where she had been watching the investigator swinging a long leg over his four-wheeler, blushing furiously at her mother's words. "No! I just hoped he would have more to tell us, that's all."

"Of course," Grace acknowledged. "So what happens now?"

"Now we wait and see what Jeff comes back with," Peter answered, coming back into the room. "There's nothing we can do until then, so we might as well get back to the lessons and know what we're doing when the harvest starts."

"Yes, and we'd better get busy in the kitchen. Carter, it's just as well you ordered so many tables—
we're going to need them all!"

"Do you think I could ask you all yet another favor? I was wondering if you'd be up for keeping a close eye on Josh tonight. I'd really like to take Kate out for dinner, and this might be our last chance before things get crazy around here."

"Tell you what," Peter answered. "We'll kill two birds with one stone. The four of us who are staying over in the other house will hang out here until you come home. Plenty of eyes to watch over Josh, and it'll give Carrie and Antonio an evening to themselves. I'll make sure he quits early today."

"And I'll prepare them a nice romantic dinner, just the two of them in their own house," Maggie interjected. Carrie smiled at her thankfully, already anticipating the evening alone with her husband, whom she'd hardly seen since their arrival.

"You know something?" Carter asked, looking around at the assembled faces. "You guys are awesome."

Chapter Thirteen

Carter and Kate sat across from each other at the restaurant table. The evening ambience was serene and romantic, with soft lighting, candles in the center of the deep burgundy tablecloths, and gentle piano music in the background. Every time he looked at her, Carter's breath caught in his throat. She was so beautiful. Her long auburn hair was spilling freely down over her shoulders, shimmering like silk in the muted half-light. Her green eyes sparkled in the flickering flame of the candle, and her signature scent of jasmine and vanilla wafted over to him every time she moved.

"You look simply stunning tonight," he told her.

She flushed and glanced down at her attire. "Oh, well, thank you. It was nice to have a reason to dress up for a change."

"I'm hoping to give you plenty of reasons to do that once this is all over."

She glanced up at him through thick, fanned lashes. "You are?"

Carter reached across the table and took her hand. "Yes, I am. Kate, I know things are a little strange right now, and we haven't had a conventional start, but I'd be honored if you would consider this our first official date. One of many."

"Then here's to first dates," she said, raising her wine glass and waiting for Carter to toast with his water glass. "So, you really want to do the whole dating thing if my…problem can be resolved?"

Carter's heart crashed to somewhere around his shoes at her question, not quick enough to stop the disappointment flashing across his face. "Not if, when. And yes, absolutely. Why, don't you?"

"Don't look so sad," she chuckled. "It's just that we seem to have gone beyond that already."

"I'm not sure I know what you mean."

"Neither am I," Kate said with a delectable little frown. "At least, I'm not sure if I can explain it. First, we were friends— close friends who shared lots about our family, our beliefs, our thinking, philosophies on life, all that stuff. We had a long time to really get to know each other as intimately as people can without actually being in a romantic relationship, you know?"

Carter nodded, understanding exactly what she meant. Back then, they had shared all that.

"Then we meet up again, and before we know it, not only have you seen into every aspect of my life, you've gotten to know my son, seen my finances, my business, the mess I'm in. You know all about my failed marriage, not to mention you're living with me right now. I just wonder how we're supposed to go back to stage one when we've pretty much covered all the rest of the stages, that's all."

Carter was worried. He couldn't help but feel she was saying things had moved so fast there were no do-overs, which they couldn't have a future because they jumped right in at the middle and never had a beginning. The problem was, he didn't entirely disagree with her, but he knew there was so much more to it than that. He had to convince her!

"Kate, it's true that we used to know everything about each other—knew what made us happy, sad, indifferent. We could pick up on each other's moods and pick out the perfect birthday gift to make each other laugh. But as people grow, they change. I still feel that getting to know you all over again will be a whole world of discovery and a journey I can't wait to take. What we're involved with right now, that's only a small part of you. It might be taking our attention, but it doesn't define either one of us. There are plenty of other sides to us that we haven't had a chance to experience and explore. I really want that chance, and believe you me, renting a room in your house is very different from actually living together as a couple. Please, don't deny us the chance of a future based on current and past events."

"I think you misunderstood me, Carter. I didn't mean that our future was in question, not in that way. What I meant was that we'd come so far already, is it really worth going right back to the beginning? I've thought a lot about you over the years, and I'm ashamed to say that even when married, I questioned how I felt about you. Once the excitement and thrill of being with someone like Joshua wore off—once I matured and understood things better—I realized that my feelings for him were nothing more than infatuation and that the far deeper feelings I had for you were the ones I should have been paying attention to all along. Having you back in my life, having you in my home, has been so wonderful. I like having you around, Carter. I like waking up knowing I'll be seeing you in the kitchen for breakfast, that you'll be with me all day in the vineyard, that we'll be having dinner together every night. It makes me feel complete, like the part of me that has been missing all these years is finally where it should be. I don't know if I can go backwards from that to seeing you once a week or whatever. That's what I meant."

"So you're saying you'd like things to move a little faster?" Carter asked, the hope in his voice undeniable.

"Just to be absolutely clear, what I'm saying is that if this is ever all over, if the business makes it after all your help if we ever get these thugs off our backs, I'd like you to stay. I don't want you to move out and go back home. I want you to stick around, my own personal hero."

Kate's eyes sparkled with unshed tears as Carter stared at her, stunned. He knew she was the woman for him—now he knew she always had been—but he hadn't dared hope she would come to the same conclusion about him so soon.

Kate took his silence as uncertainty. "Look, I know there's a lot to consider. We have to think of Josh, but he's already told me he adores you and asked if you're going to stay. Your family is fantastic, and they've been wonderful, rushing here to help. Even the two of us couldn't pull off the harvest without their help, but helping out a friend is different from accepting someone like me into the family.

"They might not like that one bit, and I'd understand. Also, I know your strong beliefs are extremely important to you, and you might not be able to accept me either. There'd be no temple wedding with me; I wouldn't be able to attend the weddings of your family and friends—that's a big deal. Gosh, listen to me talking about weddings!" Kate's pale cheeks turned a bright shade of red. "I didn't mean, well…it was just problems that popped into my head. I wasn't insinuating…."

Carter roared with laughter, delighted by her confusion and confession that she had thought about marriage. Still, he hurried to put her out of her misery. "Don't worry, I've thought about it too, and I hope marriage will be a very real possibility between us. As for my family, they love you and Josh, and they'll accept whatever and whoever I chose. We'll always have their backing, no matter what, and I'm sure they already suspect my feelings for you are deeper than just friendship. The same goes for me. I love the person you are, Kate, and that means loving every part of you."

"Carter, did you just say you loved me?"

"I did, and in case it wasn't clear, I don't just love you, I'm in love with you. Head over heels in love."

"Oh, Carter, I love you too."

The couple stared at one another, still holding hands across the table. Finally, Carter broke the silence. "I so want to kiss you right now, but this isn't the right setting."

Kate giggled. "Then it really will be like an actual first date, spending the whole evening wondering if it will end with a kiss, anticipating that, and dreaming about how it will feel."

Carter's sly, "How quickly can you eat?" brought on Kate's giggles.

***

Carter and Kate walked out to his car, arms entwined, like any pair of lovers without a care in the world. Despite Carter's teasing, they had taken their time over the meal, savoring the freedom from problems for a short while, enjoying the fine dining in the romantic setting, focused on each other. Carter would call this one of the best nights of his life, and it wasn't even over yet.

Stopping at the passenger side, he glanced around. The restaurant had been almost empty by the time they left, never wanting the evening to end. The parking lot was deserted apart from a handful of cars that probably belonged to the staff. The California evening was balmy and heavily scented with wildflowers, the night sky peppered with stars.

Carter turned Kate to face him, reveling in her beauty once more, his heart racing with anticipation. He traced her full lips with a fingertip, thrilled as she gasped and parted them slightly, tilting her head up toward him. Slowly, he ran his hand across her jawline and to the back of her neck, relishing the silky feel of her hair between his fingers. He pulled her closer with his other arm, lowering his head toward hers. He could feel his heart pounding in his chest and wondered if she could feel it too. Gently, tentatively, he touched his lips to hers, the scents and tastes of her exploding against his lips and awakening all his senses. With her response, he deepened the kiss, the world spinning around him, the years of pent up and denied emotions for this woman alone being released through his firm lips. He could feel her practically melting against him as the kiss softened again, her lips soft and yielding against his own. It felt like an eternity before they broke apart, Kate tucking her head against his chest. "I love you, Carter," she whispered.

"I love you, too," he murmured in return, kissing the silken hair on the top of her head and holding her tight.

She laughed softly. "I really am like a teenager on my first date. My legs feel wobbly."

"Then we'd better get you sitting down."

"Always my hero."

"Always," he said, giving her one final squeeze before unlocking the car door and escorting her into the passenger seat.

As he walked around to the driver's side, he thought he heard her say, "I hope so."

The drive home passed in silence, the intense, wonderful moment of their first kiss lingering with them both. Carter reached over to hold Kate's hand; she responded with an adoring smile. Neither needed idle conversation or intense discussion about their future; they were happy just to be with one another, savoring the memories of the amazing night.

All too soon, they pulled up to the large wrought iron gates that marked the entrance to Kate's property. Ever since the threats began, she had been locking them the moment the tasting room closed for the day and keeping them locked until the next morning. One of the first things she had done when Carter arrived was to give him a key. As they pulled to a halt in front of them, Kate unbuckled her seat belt.

"I'll just check the mailbox while you're getting the gates. It's been so busy; I haven't checked it for the past couple of days. No doubt it'll be full of more demands anyway, but I'd best see what I'm up against now."

She jumped back into the car clutching a large handful of mail and Carter drove through the open gates, quickly leaping out to close and lock them behind him. As they wound up the long driveway to the house, Kate leaned back in her seat and closed her eyes.

"Tired?"

"Hmm, exhausted all of a sudden."

"Must be my kissing skills," Carter joked with his usual cheekiness.

"It must be. Remind me not to kiss you again."

"No deal!"

They entered the house laughing, Kate dumping the mail on the side table in the hallway. "That lot will wait 'til morning. I'll just go and thank everybody for babysitting and say goodnight, check on Josh, then I'm going to turn in, if you don't mind."

"I don't mind, but before you do…." Carter pulled her into his arms once more, stealing one more heady kiss before joining the family.

Chapter Fourteen

Carter had just finished dressing when Kate's scream pierced the pre-dawn silence of the household. Forgoing clasping his watch as he had been about to do, he dropped it on the floor and went running in the direction of the sound, guessing it had come from the kitchen. He heard other footsteps coming from all directions—everyone was responding to the terrified sound. Charging into the kitchen, the others hot on his heels, he found Kate sitting at the kitchen table, one hand over her mouth, the other pressed against her heart.

"What's wrong?" Carter barked, ready to spring into action. With trembling fingers, Kate struggled to pick up what had scattered out over the table in front of her. After some difficulty, she held them out to Carter. Carter looked at what was in his hand, confused for a second as he recognized photographs from the last few days, all of them pictures of Josh. A smiling and laughing Josh on the front of Carter's four-wheeler, a serious-looking Josh being shown something about the grapes by Antonio, Josh walking with Grace, holding her hand and looking up at her with adoration. There were five in total, and Carter could pinpoint most of the captured moments—times when they had thought they were safe, getting on with their lives unhindered. Silently, he handed them along to Grace, whose sharp intake of breath showed she shared his shock and dismay.

"Was there any communication with them?"

Kate nodded and handed him a letter similar to the others that had been taken away by Jefferson Lakeland. Carter read it and frowned.

"Well, what does it say?" Cassie asked.

"It says 'We told you reinforcements weren't allowed. We said no one else was to get involved. You've broken the rules, and you're going to pay. The interest rate has tripled, and to make sure you got the message, we're taking the boy. Pay up or you'll never see him again…or maybe in pieces at a time.' These people are monsters! If I ever get my hands on them—"

"Calm down, Carter. Let's take time to process this. But first, Kate, where's Josh?"

"Still in bed. I haven't woken him yet."

"I'll check on him," Cassie offered. She jogged out of the kitchen and up the stairs. In only seconds, she was back, skidding into the kitchen, her face a mask of panic. "He's not there!"

"What!" Kate leapt to her feet, knocking over her chair. "They've taken him! Carter, they've got my little boy! What are we going to do?"

In the panic and confusion, Grace held up her hand and employed her business voice. "Although the timing seems a little too coincidental, we shouldn't jump to conclusions. There is every possibility that he's still on the property, so before we lose our heads, let's make sure we have our facts straight. Maggie and I will search the whole house. Nigel, go over and gather the others and split them up into areas of the vineyards after checking the guesthouse. Carter, Kate, and Cassie assign yourselves to the various outbuildings. He's a boy, and from my experience, boys like to get up to mischief and don't necessarily think through their actions, having no idea of the worry they cause by simply deciding to wander off and do something by themselves."

The family scattered to carry out their instructions, obeying Grace without a moment's hesitation. Carter grabbed Kate's hand, and they sprinted off toward the large tasting room and fermenting vats where there were plenty of places for a young boy to escape notice. The group of three split up and searched the vast barn, coming up empty-handed.

"Carter, I'll check the workers' accommodations—he's made some friends over the last few days. You check the four-wheeler shed," Cassie yelled as she sprinted off. Carter and Kate headed in that direction. Carter knew the shed was always kept locked but had no doubt that the observant, intelligent young man knew exactly where the keys were kept in the house. As they ran, they could hear voices calling for Josh in various parts of the property. Reaching the shed, they found the door hanging open, and a quick count revealed that one of the four-wheelers was missing. They glanced at each other, and Carter grabbed a set of keys off the hooks on the wall.

"Come on; I've got a feeling I know where he is."

The two of them leaped on the four-wheeler, and Carter raced down to the vines, trusting the four-wheeler to navigate the undulating ground at max speed. Kate clung tightly to him as he pushed the machine to its limits, coaxing every inch of speed from it. Carter navigated his way through the rows and rows of neat plants heavily laden with fruit, the dawn only just breaking to give him some additional, orange-hued light with which to work.

Kate kept an eye out for any sign of the small, familiar figure while Carter made his way straight to the section of the acreage that held the young white grapes. He slowed the four-wheeler as he reached the area to check their surroundings more carefully. Carter's heart lurched and Kate let out a sob as they spotted a small figure prone on the dirt among the grapes, arms by his sides, head turned to one side.

Pulling the four-wheeler to a halt, they killed the engine and jumped off, about to dash toward the figure when suddenly, it leaped to its feet with a huge grin.

"Mom, Carter, the grapes are ready, and I was the first one they told! The harvest starts today! Can I sound the horn, Mom, can I? I knew first; I'm allowed, right?"

Carter felt weak with relief, and Kate was almost choking from the effort of laughing and crying at the same time. She held out her arms and Josh ran into them, throwing his small arms around them both the best he could.

"What's wrong, Mom? Are those happy tears because you're excited about the harvest, too?"

"Yes, they're happy tears. Josh, why were you lying on the ground like that?"

"The weight of the bunch, the colors, the texture, and the tastes had all told me that the grapes were ready, just like Julian said, so I was lying on the ground listening to see if I could hear them whisper like Julian does. So I can sound the horn, right?" Josh asked, jumping back from hugs and hopping from foot to foot in his excitement.

"Yes, you can, but Josh, you shouldn't have left the house without telling someone first."

Josh's face fell, and his bottom lip began to quiver. "But I wanted to be first," he said quietly.

"I know you did, and that's great, but next time, leave me a big sheet of paper on the kitchen table with your name on it. That way I'll know you've gone out to the vines, okay?"

"Okay," he agreed, his enthusiasm returned now that he wasn't in trouble any more. Carter and Kate glanced at each other, silently communicating that there wouldn't be a next time, not at the moment. The house keys were kept hanging on a hook in the back of the kitchen, right beside the door that led to the laundry room. They were too high for Josh to reach, but he'd probably stood on a chair or something to reach them. Kate vowed that from now on, she would sleep with them under her pillow for security. Carter sent a quick text message to everyone on his family list on his phone, letting them know that Josh was fine while Kate cajoled Josh into coming back to the house for breakfast before sounding the horn.

"The workers won't be happy if we don't feed them first. Come on, I'll see if we can rustle up your favorite."

"Cheese omelets and crispy bacon?"

"Yep."

Alright!"

Carter and Josh high-fived each other, then the three of them squashed together onto the four-wheeler and drove it straight to the house, knowing they were running late for the morning meal. It took everybody working as a team to get the substantial meal on the table just as the students began to gather.

There was no time to talk, or even think, about the awful letter or the threat it posed. By the time they were all sitting down to eat, Kate had managed to compose herself and put a brave face on things for the moment. She had managed to catch a word with Julian, who had confirmed that Josh was correct, the grapes were ready. Carter tried to keep up casual conversation throughout the meal.

"Tell me, Josh, what's the horn all about?"

"It's something Dad started. You tell him, Mom," Josh replied with a mouthful of omelet.

Kate didn't have the heart to remind him of his manners this morning; she was still giddy with relief. "Yes, there were always things to signify the end of harvest—air horns, claxons, bells, fireworks, you name it—so Joshua decided to start something to mark the beginning of it, too, just for fun. Our friends and neighbors decided to pick up on it, too, and it's become a new tradition. It's a bit of a race, and the first one to begin and the first one to finish wins a prize. Just between six or seven vineyards in the area."

"What's the prize?" Carter asked.

"Bottles of wine from the other participating vineyards, of course."

"Isn't that a bit like giving snow to the Eskimos?"

"Sure," Kate laughed. "But everyone loves the chance to check out the competition for free."

"Makes sense. So tell me about the parties."

"Well, they began originally as a way to reward the staff for all their hard work and as a way of reuniting them with their families. They don't call the spouses and partners of employees grape widows for nothing. The hours are really long, and the work is really hard. It's always a relief when it's over, and it's a way of letting off steam. Of course, tourists soon wanted to be involved, so now it's a huge thing and a big draw to the area, almost like a festival. The tourists come in droves and have the chance to sample the stock and have a go at crushing grapes the old way, in a huge vat with their feet!"

"Ewww," Cassie, who was listening from across the table, interjected. "That sounds gross."

"It's not used actually to make any wine," Kate assured her. "It's just for fun. When we're sorting the grapes, any inferior bunches get kept aside for the tradition. It really gets the people involved, and our sales usually skyrocket at that time. The tourists usually want to be polite and take away stock as a thank you, and they often place advance orders and deposits for the wines from the actual harvest they attended as mementos. It's a great cash flow injection, and advance sales are always reassuring, however small."

"Sounds like a good deal all around."

"It is, and it's great fun."

Kate's face fell as she suddenly thought of something.

"What's wrong?"

"I'll have to discuss it with you later," she replied, putting a breezy smile back on her face. "Now, if everyone's finished eating, I believe we have an announcement to make to the other vineyards."

Josh cheered, and they all made their way down to the four-wheeler shed, Carter pushing the four-wheeler they had used earlier. Once gathered outside, Kate disappeared inside and reappeared with an aerosol can with a horn attached. She handed it to Josh, who promptly climbed on top of the four-wheeler's seat.

"I officially declare that our harvest has begun!" he yelled, repeating the phrase he had heard his father use in previous years.

Everyone cheered and clapped as Josh pushed the button and blasted the air horn, which echoed across the valleys. The students lifted Josh from the four-wheeler and carried him high on their shoulders toward the vines, still cheering as they went.

As they disappeared, Kade sidled up to Carter. "I've filled in those that need to know of the current situation. Myself, Julian, Nigel, Antonio, Courtney, and Chelsea are all on bodyguard duty. There'll be two of us right by Josh's side every second, spelling each other off when we have to, as there's no way to keep him from these vines today. If I were you, I'd grab Kate, Peter, and Cassie and head on back up to the house. Grace and Maggie will be heading there too. It's going to be pretty late before we can all gather to discuss it in full, so get some preliminary thoughts and ideas ready for us and take any steps you feel you need to take. You can join us down here later."

"Thanks, I'll do that," Carter said. "And Kade, can you spread the word that from now on, every door and window in both properties has to remain locked at all times? It doesn't matter if you're in or out or going between the two, we can't ignore the possibility that someone is already on the premises and might slip inside."

"You got it."

Carter carried out Kade's suggestion, and after helping the women clear away the breakfast, they sat around the kitchen table. Carter was taking a second look at the photographs.

"They could have been taken off-property with a long-range lens," he suggested. "There are plenty of places in the surrounding mountains to get an excellent view over the place."

"True, but equally they could have been taken at much closer range. Did you check out all the students?" Peter asked.

"They each came with a recommendation from their dean, and I checked their I.D. when they arrived, but I didn't have background checks run on them or anything."

"So it's possible they have someone on-site."

"We can't rule it out completely, but at least two of these were taken before the students even arrived, so I doubt any of them are responsible."

"Good point. Look, I know you're against it, Carter, but I really think we ought to have a word with the local police. Things are getting out of hand now."

"I'm afraid that if we do, they'll retaliate with violence like they said they would. I'd rather not; not until we have solid evidence that we can hand over so they can pick these guys up straight away. Can't we hang on until Jefferson comes back to us?"

Peter sighed. "Well, okay, but let it be on record that you're acting against the advice of your attorney. May I see the letter, please?"

He studied it in silence for a few moments before giving a run down. "They haven't used a single legal or business term here. The language is simplistic, and there are spelling mistakes, same as the others. Cheap paper—probably generic, buy-by-the-ream stuff available from any store, and the print looks like any run of the mill, thirty-buck inkjet printer, also readily available."

"Looks like they haven't used the clean function for a while either," Cassie added, peering over Peter's shoulder.

"Look at the pattern of lines and smudges on the paper. I'm sure they're the same as the other letters."

"That could be admissible evidence, but we'd obviously need to find the printer and prove ownership. I'd better go and give Jefferson a call, tell him what's happening, and see what he has to say. Maybe he's got good news for us at his end."

It seemed to be an eternity before Peter re-entered the room. All faces turned to him expectantly. "Good and bad," he informed them. "Firstly, he's definitely tracked down where it all began and has several credible witness statements who remember Joshua at a reputable casino in the city. The owner of the place is a big name in business with his fingers in a lot of pies—shipping companies, casinos, clubs, a brokerage firm, as well as a few restaurants and other things. In his words, everything you need to carry out just about any criminal activity and launder the money afterwards. However, he doesn't have a reputation for violence against his customers; unpaid casino debts are handled by an office-based debt collection agency and through the courts. He might be into some terrifying stuff that we don't even want to think about, and he is being closely watched by the Feds, but he doesn't send his boys out bumping off his rich clients.

"As for staff who betray him or rival gangs, they're a different matter, so we can't dismiss how dangerous and powerful he really is. He likes to keep a really low profile, though, so Jefferson is convinced that our guys are acting on their own, that they've gotten greedy over the years. The word is that the gambling place Joshua attended is owned by this guy, but he hasn't found hard evidence to prove it, only whispers from the streets. He's certain that these guys are into all sorts of things that will make their boss very unhappy, just like you suggested, Cassie. But to obtain the proof he needs, Jefferson needs to get invited to the games. He's been playing poker at the casino every night and has been winning steadily, but not enough to attract their attention yet. He's sure he will get it eventually and find everything we need to send them running for the hills, but it's going to take time. He's figured out the notebook, though, which is a record of dates, the stakes, and the losses—by the look of it, all beginning after Joshua was seen at the casino. There also seems to be some sort of code for the players, maybe a record of who he lost to on each night."

Carter suddenly had a thought. "Kate, how were you supposed to make the payment? Did you ever receive any instructions—a bank account or anything we can trace?"

"It was supposed to be in cash in a brown manila envelope marked for the attention of Sal and handed in to a coffee shop in the city. The information was in the very first communication."

"Shame there isn't something official we can use, but I guess it's something. At least we have a way of communicating with them if we decide to take a stab in the dark and fabricate a bluff. Have you ever used it to get in touch with them?"

"I haven't," Kate said. "I was going to as soon as you asked if your sister could come here. I was going to pay them whatever I could raise and ask if they could give me more time, and hold off until after the harvest just to make sure Carrie and the babies were safe. But then things kind of got hectic and I used the money I'd put aside for supplies and groceries for the students, and, well…I never got around to it."

"We can safely say it's foolproof, though. They wouldn't risk that much cash if they weren't a hundred percent certain it would reach them."

"So what do we do now?" Grace asked. "Just wait some more?"

"I'm not so sure we can afford to wait," Cassie replied, looking pointedly at the photographs. "I think we need to take more proactive action. Let me work some things out, and we'll talk again tonight. I need to make a trip into the city. Whose car can I borrow?"

Chapter Fifteen

"As I said, I'm not sure we've got the time to hang around anymore. I've got a plan, but I can tell you that most of you won't like it."

Once again the family was gathered, Cassie taking center stage. With the first day of harvest under their belts, it was time to turn their attention to the even more pressing problem they faced.

"What's the plan?" Courtney asked, leaning forward in her seat, her eyes glistening with excitement.

"Jefferson said he needed an invite to the underground games that wasn't forthcoming. He isn't coming across as a big enough gambler—not rich enough blood—so that invite might never come. These guys are looking for people with obvious affluence and a wild streak. I bet I know someone who could get that invite on the very first night."

"Oh no," Carter groaned, suspecting where this was going. "You don't mean—"

"Yep. Courtney."

"No way!" Grace and Peter had both leaped out of their seats and made the exclamation in unison. "It's far too dangerous," Grace added, with Peter nodding emphatically.

"Hold up, let's hear her out first," Courtney said, delighted at the prospect of some real excitement.

"The way I see it, these guys are looking for something particular—someone who isn't afraid to take risks at the card table, indicating they're willing to take risks in life. Someone who's a little flashy with their cash, a big tipper, not afraid to put their money where their mouth is. Someone who thinks they're hot stuff. Who better than a sexy, mysterious woman dripping with bling and playing a mean game?"

"I could totally play that role," Courtney suggested enthusiastically.

"We all could play a similar role of a high roller. Why can't I do it, or some of the other guys?" Carter asked.

"For one, you're in the photographs, so they know who you are. If you're seen anywhere near that casino, they'll know we've made a connection, and we risk tipping them off. We have to assume they've seen all of us, but the advantage women have is that they can very easily make themselves look totally different. The second thing is, sorry bro, but I bet you couldn't win a hand of poker to save your life."

"I guess you've got me there. Can you play, Courtney?"

"You bet I can! Texas Hold 'Em, Five Card Stud, Midnight Baseball—you name it, I can play it. How else do you think teenagers spend their time when they're hanging around drinking beer after football season is over? Besides, it was one of the many useful life skills David Fisher thought it important to teach me."

Everyone ignored the sarcasm of the last statement (aimed at the man who, until recently, Courtney had believed to be her real father; he was a topic of conversation best left unspoken). Carter was beginning to look thoughtful.

"Okay, so let's say this works and Courtney gets the invite. What then?"

"Right, so she gets the invite to join in the next underground game. She goes along, wins for a while, then starts to lose. Still, she shows no fear and doesn't hold back or get cautious. Finally, she's out of cash, so she asks for a marker. Maybe they take her through to the office, maybe they don't, but she'd need to speak to someone in charge, right? Then she can ask questions about how soon she has to pay, what happens if she can't, that kind of thing. Establish the terms. With a bit of luck, something incriminating will come up, or at the very least something we can use to give weight to any scam they try to pull. All the time she's there, she's got a hidden video camera in a clutch purse, you know, like the ones they use on those whistleblower documentaries?"

"You're talking about entrapment and recording without consent. None of this would be admissible as evidence in a court of law," Peter pointed out.

"Would I actually be breaking the law by doing it?" Courtney asked.

Peter made a face. "It's still a bit of a gray area, getting worse by the technology easily available nowadays, and it varies from state to state. It's not a federal offense, but the other party can file a civil lawsuit, which would then be tried in a court of law. The court would have to decide whether the conversation was intended to be confidential. If it took place on a telephone or in a private residence, then you're definitely breaking the law, but if you were recording a conversation that could be overheard, like in a restaurant or on the sidewalk, then generally no."

"So in this case, if it took place in front of more than one person, and it's not a house, which is unlikely, then you would feel, as a lawyer, that I wasn't committing a criminal act by recording the conversation for my own purposes?"

"I would certainly be confident of winning the case for my client."

"Good enough to satisfy me ethically," Courtney grinned at him. "So what does everybody think?"

"I still think it's too dangerous," Grace said.

"Not a problem, Mom. There'll be two of us. I intend to go along, too, just two girls out for a night of fun. Nigel, will you drive us and wait for us?" Cassie replied.

"Of course."

"See Mom? Nigel will be waiting for us. Any trouble and we scamper. He'll whisk us away to safety."

"I'd give Jefferson a heads-up on the plan. He can keep an eye on you in the main casino, but once you get the invite, you'll be on your own, girls."

"Peter, don't tell me you're seriously considering giving this craziness your blessing?" Grace said, shocked at the one person she thought she could rely on to put an end to this discussion.

Peter rubbed his face with his hands. "I don't know. I don't want either of them in danger, but I can see how set they are on the idea. Besides, I'm pretty sure they'll be absolutely fine on the first night in the regular casino, especially with Jefferson around. They might not even get the invite, or maybe not before he does. I think we have to let them at least go through with that. If I don't back the idea, Courtney might never forgive me."

The couple smiled at each other, a wealth of mutual understanding and love passing between them. "I still have two questions, though. You girls are going to be gambling. Can you reconcile that within yourselves?"

"I've been wrestling with that internally throughout this discussion," Courtney replied. "The way I see it is we're not doing it for gain; we're not even doing it for fun. We have a cause, and it's a good one. It's a means to an end, a way of hopefully finding a solution. That's got to count for a lot, but then I'm the newest member of the church here. What does everyone else think?"

"Gambling's a sin, so you shouldn't do it," Maggie said.

"It won't be the only rule we'll be breaking," Cassie reminded them. "We'll be dressed inappropriately, decked out in ostentatious finery, and using our femininity to achieve our goals. It's only going to be for a few nights at most, and we'll be playing a role, including the gambling. No one would bat an eyelid at it if we were actresses. I think the cause outweighs the deed in this case. We're not hurting anyone; we aren't going to cheat or steal. All we want is to put the fear of God into some gangsters."

"You could try converting them instead," Peter, the returned missionary, joked. They all laughed, breaking the tension in the room. "I say we take a vote on it or we could be discussing it for hours."

They all agreed. Grace, Maggie, Kade, and Kate all voted against, for their own personal reasons and beliefs. Cassie, Courtney, Peter, and Antonio all voted in the positive, leaving it tied four apiece.

"Nigel?" Cassie asked.

"Sorry love," he said with an apologetic look at his wife. "Yes."

"Chelsea?"

"I'm sorry, both of you, but I have to stand with Kade on this one. I couldn't bear it if something happened to one of my sisters. If these men can threaten the life of a six-year-old, they'd have no trouble harming either of you. I've lost enough people that I love. It has to be no."

"So we're tied again with two votes left. What do you say, Carrie?"

"I know I'm the eldest and I should be the most sensible one. My head's telling me there are a million reasons why I should say no, but this amazing woman and her wonderful son deserve everything we can do for her, and so does our brother. I want it noted, though, that my vote for now only applies to the main casino. I motion that we discuss things again should the invite be forthcoming. With that said, I have to follow the way my heart is being pulled and say yes. If Antonio believes it could amount to something that can help, then I say go for it."

Cassie turned to Carter. "Looks like you have the power to swing it for the ayes or tie the vote again."

All eyes were on him as he considered his answer. "I wish some of us could go with you, or better yet, go in your place, but everything you've said makes sense. I'm with Carrie, though—this only applies to the initial idea. I say yes."

"Now that everything's decided, that brings me to my next question," Peter reminded them. "Where do we get the surveillance equipment?"

"Way ahead of you," Cassie said with excitement. "I didn't just spend my shopping day fawning around in high-end couture and exclusive jewelry shops, although that was a large part of it. I also spent quite a while in an electronics shop. A very helpful guy sold me everything I could possibly need and was probably able to take the rest of the day off on the commission."

Cassie dove behind the sofa and produced armfuls of bags displaying some of the best known designer names. She hunted until she found the one from the electronics store. "Look at these," she proudly declared, holding up two Gucci clutch purses. "He installed these tiny cameras in them for me. It's no bigger than a pin head and wirelessly streams to this unit here so you can record audio and video without having a bulky device on you. I got the ones with the best range, so I'm hoping it will be good enough to do it from the car. I thought the purses would be best, as we can control the angle of the camera by holding them, laying them down—whatever's needed. We've got these ear piece things, and goodness knows what else. I have to admit, I lost interest, but I'm sure you guys will sort it all out for us."

"I'm more interested in what's in the other bags," Courtney grinned.

"Help me carry them upstairs, and you can have a peek. The rest of you will have to wait until tomorrow night. I want you to get the full effect and confirm that we've been transformed!"

The girls disappeared, leaving the others staring at each other.

"Someone, please tell me we've done the right thing," Carter groaned.

None of them could. All Kate could do was squeeze his hand reassuringly.

Chapter Sixteen

Carter, Peter, Courtney, and Chelsea had begged off chores at 4 p.m. the next day in order to make final arrangements for that night's excursion. Nigel was outside polishing and buffing the car to a high shine, while the girls were upstairs doing goodness knew what. Carter and Peter sat at Kate's kitchen table; the electronic equipment spread out before them. Carter had been the one who had stayed up to figure out the bag of tricks after the others had retired to bed. He was now explaining what he had learned to Peter.

"Whatever the camera and microphone pick up gets wirelessly streamed back to this main receiver. It's fitted with a memory card, so you have the option to watch live or hit record."

"It could be a long night; how long can it record for?"

"It came with an average-sized SD card, but either Cassie knows more than she lets on or that salesman was really thorough. There was a pair of the latest 12 TB cards in there, too. I've already swapped them over, and just in case, there are extra memory sticks too. I've been over all this with Nigel early this morning, but I've had a few thoughts that I wanted to run by you."

"Go ahead," Peter said.

"Nigel can be watching everything happening inside live on the screen. Couldn't there be a couple of us in the car so we can respond if the girls get into any trouble?"

Peter immediately shook his head. "No. I don't think he should watch the screen. The one thing every casino has is an abundance of hi-tech security; even the parking lot will be covered from a million different angles. They could, in theory, decide to zoom in to see what's Nigel's watching, just out of curiosity or boredom. It could be disastrous if they realize he's watching a recording of inside the casino. He can listen, but the screen has to stay flipped down. Also, one smartly dressed, bored-looking guy listening to headphones after dropping off two party girls from an expensive car just screams personal driver. More people in the car waiting for them screams suspicious. You could put the girls in danger just by drawing attention to them."

Carter looked disappointed but accepted Peter's judgment. "Okay then. How about...." Carter glanced apologetically over to Maggie, who was helping Grace with the preparations for a light, early supper for the girls and Nigel. "Sorry, no offense, but Nigel's a little slower than he used to be. How about one of us plays the role of chauffeur instead?"

"No offence taken, Carter. I'm well aware that we're not spring chickens anymore," Maggie said with a chuckle. "But I think Cassie asked Nigel for a specific reason, so I wouldn't interfere with your sister's crazy scheme too much if I were you."

"What reason's that?" Carter asked, looking curious.

Maggie mimicked sealing her lips. "Not my secret to tell. Ask Nigel."

The men glanced at each other and shrugged. "He's perfect anyway—he has the bearing of a close personal employee of someone very rich," Peter said.

"You mean the worn-down look of someone used to running around trying to keep tabs on a brat used to getting her own way," Maggie joked.

Grace chuckled to herself. She knew her children weren't spoiled, but she also knew they all looked upon Maggie and Nigel as a second set of parents and had often given them the same hard time as they had given her and John when they were small. They'd tried the usual tricks of playing them against each other, getting something out of one that they had been refused from the other. There was no doubt that all five of them had been hard work in their own ways.

"Okay, so what about these ear pieces?" Peter asked.

"Well, there are two pairs, so I've calibrated them all to the same frequency. They're similar to the Bluetooth headsets you can pair with a smartphone, only so discrete they can't be seen. It means whatever is said can be heard by others, like a continual party call. The girls will each have one in case they're separated for any reason. After they've been in there a couple of hours, giving them time to pretend to have a drink or two, get their chips, wander around and play a few games like tourist gamblers, getting the lay of the place before choosing a poker table, Nigel will go in to use the men's room. Jefferson will follow him, and Nigel will slip him one of these, so he's in the loop. Everyone has been warned that others could tap into the frequency so not to say anything incriminating if they can help it. I'd hoped the other could be for one of us in the car, but I guess it's just a spare now. Nigel will be listening to the audio from the cameras so that he won't need it."

"We'd better go and get this installed in the car."

The men gathered up the receiver and went outside. Grace and Maggie looked at each other uneasily. "I'm still not happy about this," Grace commented.

"I know, neither am I, but they seem to be taking every possible precaution. All we can do is pray that the girls stay safe. We can pray together if you like after they've gone."

Grace put a hand on her old friend's shoulder. "Thanks, Maggie, I'd like that very much."

***

At 6:30 pm, the clatter of high heels on the tiled corridor alerted them that the girls were ready. The two women who entered the kitchen were barely recognizable, and Carter stared at them in amazement, wondering where his sisters had gone. Both of them were dressed in figure-hugging black couture dresses. Courtney's had off-the-shoulder sleeves and barely covered the tops of her thighs, while Cassie's was sleeveless and full-length but plunged at the neck line and the back, with a revealing slit up one side. Both were wearing sheer black stockings and killer black heels with bright red soles that flashed as they walked. Cassie's normally dirty blonde, disheveled, thick hair was a lighter shade, brushed until it shone and swept up into a high up-do, with curled tendrils left loose to frame her face. Courtney's jet black pixie cut was now long, inky black tresses that reached down to the small of her back. Both wore heavy make-up, but rather than being trashy, it was dark and smoky and looked expertly applied. Their outfits were finished off by jewelry that said it lived in a bank vault and was only taken out for special occasions. Cassie's platinum earrings, necklace, and bracelet were studded with the highest clarity diamonds and emeralds that flashed the same rich green as her eyes. Courtney's set was gold, with a mixture of white and black diamonds, setting off her dark looks perfectly. Both also sported heavy, expensive watches, and Carter shuddered to think of the cost of Cassie's extreme shopping trip.

Cassie giggled at the expressions on their faces that stared at them. "Well, do we look like a couple of wild, rich party girls bored with our life and looking to take some risks?"

"Absolutely! More to the point, I hardly recognize you both, so anyone who saw you around here would never put two and two together."

"Provided they're not being watched as they leave," Grace added.

Everyone glanced at each other. They hadn't thought of that, and judging by the recent photographs, they'd been watched far more often than they'd thought. They all considered the possibility in silence as Grace served up the light snacks she had prepared for them. The girls ate slowly, careful not to ruin their lipstick.

"Maybe if we use the cellar," Kate suddenly declared. Everyone turned to look at her. "Off the utility room, there's another door that leads to an underground stone cellar—the original wine store. It has another set of steps that leads up to the outside hatch doors. They're right around the back of the property, shielded from the road by the house, hidden from the mountains by the outbuildings, and there are quite a few large bushes on either side. If Nigel could navigate the car around there and up close, they could slip into the back seat and stay down until he's away from here. I've got a couple of shawls they can borrow to cover their hair and shoulders, just as an extra precaution."

"Perfect," Nigel said. "I'll take a quick look, but I'm sure it'll be no problem."

"I wouldn't do it in those heels, though; the stone steps will be treacherous," Kate joked, lightening the mood again now that the problem was solved.

"I can't say I'm too fond of your outfits, girls, but Cassie, it's nice to see your hair looking so good," Grace commented.

Cassie laughed. "I know, right? It's just one of those blonde-enhancing shampoo and conditioners. It promised to work after just one wash, and it seems to have delivered. Doesn't Courtney look amazing with long hair? They're extensions, but you'd never know. I had to have a lesson on how to fit them, as well as tutorials from the make-up counter. Maybe I should have had lessons in how to walk in heels, too!"

"You should take some pictures of us—we'll never look like this again in our lives," Courtney added. "Unless we decide to join the FBI and do undercover work."

Grace shuddered at the thought but entered into the spirit, taking pictures of the girls and keeping the upbeat mood, hiding her worry and concern. She knew that despite their playfulness, they would remember the seriousness of what they could be getting into and do their best to stay safe and focused on their task. She trusted them to use their intelligence. She had to admit that she was relieved Courtney was with Cassie. Her earlier life had given her a level of street smarts that the sheltered Cassie would lack. Once the girls had gone, all the rest of them could do was pray, wait, and worry.

***

The house was shrouded in darkness when the three returned, everyone having gone to bed as normal in case the house was under surveillance. Any break from the standard routine would be suspicious. Nigel dropped the girls off at the back cellar door before parking the car nearby at the side of the house, giving himself a viable reason for reversing into that section of the grounds. He then let himself in the front door, waving goodnight to the girls as they tiptoed up the stairs in their stocking soles, flushed and excited about their adventure now that they were home…and safe. In order not to disturb both households, Courtney was sleeping over with Chelsea in her room tonight. Grace, with a mother's highly tuned ears, was finally able to turn over and go to sleep as she heard the hushed whispers of the girls discussing their night as they got ready for bed. Maggie, too, was finally able to rest easy as her husband slipped under the covers beside her.

Chapter Seventeen

Anxious to hear the story of last night, the whole family was up long before they needed to be, sitting around Kate's table yet again, drinking orange juice to try to wake up after their late, restless night. Cassie was keen to tell them the highlights of the events.

"Courtney was amazing! She played her skills down, making a few small wins, then a few loses, lulling everyone into a false sense of security, then boom! She bid them all up and took a massive pot! She played it down so that she was as surprised as everyone else like it was just sheer dumb luck. Quite a crowd had gathered to watch, and everyone was applauding and congratulating her. Even the manager came around with a bottle of champagne to say congratulations. We didn't drink any, naturally, but Courtney shared it with the others, and no one noticed. We kept the bottle, of course, in case it could be of any use. It's got some fancy, personalized label for the casino. Could be a clue."

"We can pass it to Jefferson, see if he makes anything of it," Peter agreed.

"It wasn't long after that she was approached by a guy asking her if she would like to play for higher stakes. She played it perfectly, and she was handed this, and instructions to be at this address at 10 pm tomorrow night!"

Cassie proudly displayed the business card—the same one that Joshua had tucked into his pocket, with the same handwriting scrawled across the back.

"I'm not sure, but I raised my purse as high as I could to tuck the card into, so I think I might have gotten his face on camera. There were also some interesting conversations going on at the table I was playing at. I think we got some great information, and with the invite, I would say phase one of the mission was most definitely achieved," Courtney added with a grin.

"Well done, girls. You did really well. We can't thank you enough for the effort you put in," Carter said.

"Do you think you've got enough so that we don't have to take this any further?" Grace asked.

"We can't stop now, Mom—not when we've gone this far! We have to go along tonight and finish this."

"I was afraid you were going to say that."

"I think the fact that they got their invite means they played their cover beautifully. I think they could push it one more night, but that would be it," Peter added.

"If it was going back to the casino, I would agree, but this is going to somewhere unknown, where there won't be any bystanders."

"Nigel will be there within range, and no doubt Jefferson will be hanging about as close as possible, trying to see if he can get a signal on the earpiece. Did all that go down the way it should?"

"Yep, all went as planned," Nigel answered Peter.

"See, Mom? We'll be fine."

"I guess you're going to do it regardless, with or without my blessing. You're both grown women, although you'll always be my little girls. Better that I'm in on everything than you having to sneak around trying to keep things from me."

"You're the best mom ever!"

"Funny how all my kids say that when they're getting their own way," Grace smiled wryly.

"Right, plans for the day. Cassie, can you upload the file from the memory card and send it to Jefferson? I also think we should transcribe it so we have a hard copy. We might want to take sections out to compose our little package, instructed Carter.

"Oh, can I do that? It'll give me something to do and make me feel like part of the action. I love these babies, but they sure are making me miss out on the fun," Carrie joked.

"Fine, that's settled then. Cassie, can you also see if you can print stills from the video file? Any mug shots of the people at the table, the manager, and our mysterious friend. Any problems with that, just give me a call and I'll come and see what I can do."

"Sure, Peter, no problem."

Grace glanced at the clock on the wall. "We'd better get breakfast started. The students will be up soon."

***

"One chance only. Let's give it all we've got," Cassie muttered to Courtney as they walked together up to what looked like an abandoned building on the wrong side of town.

Nigel had found a spot to park nearby close enough to get a strong signal from the wireless cameras. There was no sign of Jefferson Lakeland, but Cassie had the feeling he would be lurking around somewhere.

"You bet," Courtney replied as they stepped up to the door and double checked the number. "This is it."

They knocked and waited.

The door was opened by a heavily tattooed bear of a man, his head shaved to the bone and gleaming in the sickly yellow streetlights.

"Hi," Courtney said brightly. "We're here by invitation."

"Card?" the man grunted.

Courtney lifted her purse to fish out the card, capturing the presumed bouncer on film. She showed it to him, and he nodded, opening the door wider to let them pass.

"Third floor, second door on the right," was all he said. He made no move to escort them further into the premises.

The girls walked along the corridor, their high heels echoing across the bare wooden floor. There was nothing remaining to indicate what this building might once have been. No fixtures or fittings lingered; everything had been ripped out. The walls were covered by a dull gray peeling and flaking paint and light fittings were bare bulbs hanging from plastic coated wires. The place was a four-story labyrinth, scuffed doors leading off the main corridor in both directions. Each room they passed that had an open door was empty and devoid of life or purpose. At the end of the corridor sat a bare, winding wooden staircase with an old-fashioned iron and wood handrail. They began to climb, and the stairs creaked and groaned under their weight. They glanced at each other, saying nothing as they ascended further into the gloom.

Reaching the third floor, they could hear voices—faint murmurings, all in male tones. They each took a deep breath, plastered bright, vacant smiles on their faces, and knocked on the instructed door.

"Come."

They entered. Courtney's eyes flashed quickly around the room, taking in her surroundings. The door had opened into the center of a room just as gloomy as the rest. To her left was a makeshift bar, rough wooden shelves stocked with mostly whisky as far as she could tell. To her right was a high-end ten-seat tournament-grade poker table, the deep burgundy felt and gleaming mahogany rail seeming out of place in the derelict surroundings. Several men were already seated there, drinks and ashtrays balanced on the rail beside them. All eyes appraised the women as they walked in, taking in their appearance from head to toe, lingering over certain areas that almost made Cassie blush. She kept herself in check, knowing that the people they were pretending to be would be used to this sort of scrutiny. She had her purse tucked up under her arm, and she turned and looked around the room instead, allowing the camera to take it all in. The man seated with his back to the bar and his right side facing toward the door rose from his seat.

"Welcome, ladies. Thank you for coming. I hope you brought your A-game. We're waiting for one other gentleman, and then we can begin. May we offer you some refreshments?"

"Oh no, I'm good, thanks. If we drink any more, we might be under the table instead of at it." The girls giggled, and the man's face flashed annoyance before he covered the expression. "Where do you want me to sit?" Courtney continued innocently as if she had totally missed the disapproval.

"Anywhere you like," he replied, indicating the four free seats.

"And where do I get my chips?" she asked as she took a seat on the door side of the table. It was in her peripheral vision to her left, and she felt better knowing she had quick access to it.

"First, the rules. No getting drunk, no getting rowdy—this is a serious game. $5,000 buy-in, no limits Texas Hold 'Em. House takes 20% of each pot at the end of the night. No cell phones; hand them over before we begin. Agreed?"

Courtney clapped her hands. "Oh, goody, Texas Hold 'Em is such fun! Good luck with the 20%, though. If my math is right—and I have to admit it wasn't my best subject—20% of nothing is nothing," she giggled. "I don't think I'll win a thing."

She could see the other men at the table glance at each other. Some smirked, and some rolled their eyes, wondering exactly what had been brought into their high-stakes game. One of them pointedly raised an eyebrow at the man in charge, who shrugged in return.

"See the gentleman at the bar to pay your dues and get your chips."

A quick glance at the piles on the table in front of each player told Courtney exactly how much was normal. At the bar, she noted that the guy there wasn't the man who had invited her to the game, meaning there were at least three of them involved. She turned off both their cell phones and handed them over, paid the buy-in fee, and asked for double the number of chips of the biggest pile in the room so far, handing over an obscene amount of cash. She saw the flashes of greed that crossed the faces of her companions. She felt the mood in the room lift as they considered how much they were going to make off this flake in their midst.

After taking her place back at the table, Cassie inquired of the men sitting there, "Since you've got so many, can I have some of those? I fancy playing tonight. You, gentlemen, don't mind if I join in, do you?" she asked, swiveling her body to look at each one in turn.

"Be my guest," the man directly across leered. "A pretty view makes for a nice change around here."

They all chuckled, and Cassie took her place next to Courtney, who casually pushed a large pile of chips her way. Another knock came at the door, and once the final player was settled, the game was underway. The players were cautious at first, trying to get a feel for their opponents, seeing if they could figure out their tills and keeping the bets relatively conservative. Courtney won and lost a few hands, and Cassie lost every time with a good-natured shrug. After the first hour, the game took a more serious turn, the antes increasing substantially, and Cassie was almost out of chips. Scrapping her way to the big blind, she looked at her cards, shrugged again, and threw in all her remaining pile.

"I don't even know how much each of these is worth—they don't feel like real money anyway! Is that enough to keep me in?"

"Sure, Cutie, unless anyone else ups the bid," the man across from her answered.

The players each took their turns, some folding, some calling. In the reveal, Cassie had two low pairs—a hand easily beaten by another player. "Oh, well, guess I'm out, but it was fun!" she said as the winner raked in the pile of chips from the center.

"Take your seat back from the table if you're sticking around," the leader said. "In the corner over there."

"Oh, sure, I won't get in the way."

Cassie did as she was told, sitting in the corner and looking bored. Her admirer glanced at her several times and grinned at her as the game progressed. Several hours later, they were two players down, having lost everything and left after refusing a marker for borrowed funds, much to the disappointment of the man at the bar. Cassie had the whole thing on camera. Seeing that Courtney appeared to be up on her winnings and a couple of other players had their stacks of chips drastically reduced, Cassie got to her feet before the next deal.

"Say, guys, is there a bathroom in this place?"

"Fifth door on the left down the corridor," the head man answered, not taking his eyes off the table.

"Don't expect it to be a throne, princess," the man at the bar added with a derisive laugh, letting the women know exactly what he thought of them.

Cassie suspected that if it hadn't been for the number of chips Courtney had purchased, they would have been thrown out before the game got serious. She'd made the right call, even though the plan was to lose it all. She exited the room and made sure her high heels could be heard stomping down the hall until she reached the bathroom. Tiptoeing her way back up the corridor, she checked each room as she went.

Finally, she found what she was looking for. One room was set up as an office, with a computer desk, a large safe, a couple of gray metal file cabinets, and a computer with a cheap printer sitting beside it. The computer was already running, a screen saver playing across the screen. Hoping it didn't ask for a password, she slipped behind the desk and moved the mouse, relieved that the home page came up with icons and a generic background picture. Fingers flying, she opened a social media site, typed in a random name, and scanned through the search results, narrowing them until she found a young woman whose hometown wasn't far outside San Francisco. Finding nothing in the posts she could use, she tried again, using the friend's link to search another.

Back in the room, Courtney wondered what Cassie was up to, having deviated from the plan to always stick together. In her earpiece, she could hear what she thought was the hum of a computer tower and the clicking of a mouse. She began to get nervous—Cassie had been gone too long. She heard the distinct sound of an inkjet printer starting up in her ear just as the man at the bar marched out of the room, presumably in search of Cassie. Courtney considered her options. She could say something to warn her, knowing Cassie would hear her on her earpiece, but it would look suspicious to the people in the room. They might search them, discovering the earpieces and the cameras. No, she had to trust that Cassie had worked out a cover story before taking her chances. Courtney would just have to go with the flow. She tried to keep her face expressionless and her attention on the game as she heard a voice in her ear.

"What the hell do you think you're doing?"

Within seconds, the bartender burst back into the room, holding Cassie roughly by the top of her arm. The man in charge of the game glanced around impatiently. "What are you doing with our guest, Dean?"

The man looked in slack-jawed amazement as if stunned someone would be so careless as to use his name in front of the players. "Well, *Sal*," he emphasized, tit for tat, "I caught her snooping around the office."

Cassie looked indignant. "I already told you, I wasn't snooping. You took my phone, and I wanted to check my social media. You see, Brad was going out with Lucy, but Celia told him that Lucy had met with an old flame from college for coffee and Brad was jealous so he dumped Lucy, see? So then Brad starts going out with Gloria, but he told Ivan that he was only doing it to make Lucy jealous, that he was still in love with her and wanted her back. So then Ivan tells Blake, and Blake tells Simon and well, Simon, he's a blabbermouth and can't keep anything to himself, so he messages Gloria, but rather than be mad at Brad, she gets mad at Lucy and posts on her wall that—"

"Shut up!" Dean roared. "You're making my ears bleed. You dang rich valley chicks are all the same, no lives outside of gossip."

"This is what you interrupted our game for?" Sal asked.

"She was using the printer too, boss," Dean mumbled.

Sal's eyes narrowed. "Tell me, dear, what was it you were printing?"

"Oh, it's totes amazeballs. Veronica posted this hilariously bitchy comment, and I knew Jenny wouldn't believe me until she saw it, so I had to print it, 'cause, like, we could be here for hours and...."

Sal held out his hand, and Cassie handed over the sheet of paper. He looked at the three-sentence comment from a social media page and snorted, practically throwing the piece of paper back to Cassie, who caught it and folded it quickly into her purse.

"You shouldn't have gone wandering around without permission."

"Well, geez, it's only a computer, and I only borrowed it for a second," Cassie said with an air of someone no one ever refused.

"I think it's time for you girls to leave."

"Oh, but I've only just gotten started," Courtney exclaimed. "It was only a little misunderstanding."

"Yeah, let the girls stay," one of the players added. "Give us a chance to win our money back."

The others laughed, but Sal shook his head. "House reserves the right to say who plays, and I say these two are done. It's past your bedtime, ladies. Time to go home."

The men watched wistfully as Courtney and Cassie gathered up the pile of chips and carried them over to the bar to cash in. Dean handed over the cash—substantially more than Courtney had cashed in at the beginning—with a sour look. "Two of you played, so I'm keeping two lots of buy-ins. This is less the extra five grand and the 20%."

Courtney knew by the stacks that he had shorted her, but she was still well up, and she didn't dare argue and delay their escape. Still, she took her time packing the money into her purse then tucking it high under her arm. She had to pass some bundles and their phones to Cassie; it wouldn't all fit back into her purse. She took a final sweep of the room. "It was nice to meet you all. Maybe we'll get a rematch sometime!"

With a little wave, the two of them stalked out of the room, still pretending to be offended they had been kicked out of such a lowly establishment. They resisted the urge to speed up as they made their way back down the flights of stairs. They walked in silence, not knowing how far their voices would carry. Arriving on the last flight of steps, they ran into the guy who had originally invited them to the game.

"Hi, ladies, leaving so soon?"

"Yeah, game's a bust for us," Courtney shrugged, trying to sound as if they had both lost.

"Shame. Maybe next time, eh?" the man replied with a happy grin, thinking of the takings from the pretty rich girls. He'd seen exactly how much cash she had been flashing the night before. He all but rubbed his hands together with glee.

"Sure, next time," they agreed with a little wave, taking the rest of the steps a little faster. They made their way past the bouncer, who held the door open for them. As soon as it closed behind them, the car screeched up alongside, and they dove in, Nigel taking off before they had barely sat down. He'd only reached the end of the street when he looked in the rearview mirror, spotting the door being flung open again.

"Thought as much," he said. "Buckle up, girls—they're going to try and tail us. I think they might want that money back, and since they couldn't win it, they've decided just to steal it."

"Now that really isn't fair. They got their buy-in fee and their 20%."

"Must just be too much to pass up on. Either that or they're beginning to suspect there was something more going on here. Hold on."

It was after 3 am, and the city streets were almost deserted. Nigel took full advantage, having been studying maps since his arrival, getting the layout of the city. He twisted and turned, ducked and weaved through tiny side alleys, floored it up and down never-ending hills, handling the car expertly around every tight bend and curve. Only once there hadn't been any vehicles behind him for more than twenty minutes did he make his way over to exit the city and head for home, ensuring he didn't pick up a tail on the way. Once well out of the city, he slowed down to within the speed limit.

"What on earth was that?" Courtney asked. "Nigel, did you used to be a fed or something?"

"No, just a NASCAR driver," he grinned in the rearview mirror.

"Ha ha, very funny."

"He's not kidding," Cassie giggled. "Before he got married, he was beginning to make quite a name for himself. If he'd kept it up, he would have been a household name to all his fans by now."

Courtney stared at Cassie in astonishment. "You knew about this?"

"Known for years," Cassie replied smugly. "Came across his name during research for a novel."

"And you kept it to yourself?"

"Of course. Nigel hadn't said anything, so I figured it wasn't my secret to tell. I had to tell him that I knew, though."

"So why did you give it up?" Courtney asked directly to the dark horse himself.

"Just figured that if I was to make an honest woman of Maggie and have a family, I should be more responsible and look for a safer career."

Courtney mulled that over while Cassie had a thought. "Hey, do you think they saw the car? They might spot it at the house and put two and two together."

"I think they'll be making the connection once we get in touch with everything we have anyway, but I'd already thought of that. After I drop you both home, we'll all check the house to be sure it's safe. Then I'm heading out to the airport to the 24/7 rental place and swapping it for something else. If I'm lucky, they'll have something even faster."

"Good call. Nigel. Hey, Courtney, what are you going to do with all those winnings? They weren't part of the plan."

"I know! Their loss, since they didn't let us stay until I'd lost it all. I'll get to keep my original stake, but I've already decided the rest is going to charity."

"Maybe there's a buy-a-fast-car-for-retired-racing-drivers fund?" Nigel asked hopefully.

The three of them laughed and the girls relaxed back in their seats, knowing they had a lucky escape and that things had gone as well as they could have expected under the circumstances.

Chapter Eighteen

Jefferson Lakeland turned up the next day just in time for breakfast. He pulled up a chair at the end of the table and happily made himself at home among the students vying for the huge array of serving dishes lined up along the center of the tables, causing them to creak and groan under their weight. It was a reduced crew that went to work in the fields, as the entire family gathered to see what he had to say. All the information had been sent to him in the early hours of the morning, and he was here to give his report. Moving inside, they all settled down and waited for him to begin.

"Well, you've all been pretty busy, haven't you?" Jefferson said. "I want you to know it was a pretty dumb thing to do considering how dangerous these wise guys are, but I have to say, I admire the guts it took and the way you kept your cool when it started to go south."

Jefferson stared at Courtney and Cassie, whom he recognized from each other's cameras and knew to be the women who had placed themselves in danger to gather information. Cassie flushed pink under his appraisal, looking pleased and embarrassed at the same time.

"We've got quite a lot to go on now. While you were out gallivanting last night, I had an invite of my own, only mine was quite different. I was invited by the manager of the casino himself, had two hours' notice, and the game was held in some huge mansion. I won't disclose the location. Everything was laid on, and although the buy-in was five times what you paid, there was no cut to the house from your pot. That isn't standard practice among these gentleman thieves. I didn't stick around for long, made a show of losing and bowing out, and nobody offered me a loan—only commiserations and better luck next time. So boss man is running his own illegal games, and I'm pretty sure he knows nothing about what his goons are up to on the side.

"The building you visited is owned by him, but it's earmarked for conversion to office space within the next year. The coffee shop isn't owned by him. The owner was happy to talk in confidence in exchange for the slightest chance of getting Sal off his back. He's being coerced, and not in a nice way, to use his place as Sal's personal laundry room. After I left the game last night, I headed over your way. I saw you girls leave and that they tried to follow but failed. Nice driving, by the way."

Nigel acknowledged the compliment but said nothing. Cassie took the break in Jefferson's flow to clarify matters.

"So if we prepare a small package with lots of stills of them, from being approached at the casino right up to the coffee shop itself, write them a note saying we have evidence of their illegal games, the buy-in fees, the pot dues, and the coercion they're using to chase up a marker from a widow, and that not only are we going to present it to their boss, but we're going public with it on the front page of a highly esteemed newspaper, they'd back off?"

"I'm pretty sure they'd do more than back off; they'd run for their lives. Even if the boss were in on the deal, he would be in for the buy-ins only, not the 20% extra, and I'd stake my life he knows nothing of the money being laundered at the coffee shop. Not only would he want them dead for their betrayal, but also for dragging his name into the limelight, which is somewhere he definitely doesn't want to be."

"Yes!" Cassie exclaimed. "We've got them! It's a pity I didn't have longer at that computer. I wanted to prove they owned the printer by matching up those ink marks, but if I'd had the time, I'd have gone searching for their books. Both sets—the cooked one for their boss and the real one. That would have really sealed the deal, not to mention giving the police enough to pick them up."

"I think we might have enough for that to happen anyway, but if they get picked up here, they're dead men," Peter said. "We have to decide what we want to do about that."

The room went silent. They hadn't considered what would happen to the men if their boss actually discovered their betrayal.

"Surely they would be safe serving a prison sentence?" Grace asked.

"Not a chance," Jefferson replied. "This man more or less runs this city, both on the outside and the inside. I'd give them a week before they were knockin' on St. Peter's door."

"Then I think we have to give them every opportunity to run," Carter said. "How far would they go?"

Jefferson shrugged. "If they've got any brains at all, they'll not only get out of state but out of the country. Maybe Mexico, maybe Canada; it depends how far the crews' connections go."

"But if they're free, won't they just start up again? Can we, in all good conscience, allow them to do this to someone else?" Grace asked, ever the voice of reason.

"No, I guess we can't," Carter sighed. "Does anyone have any ideas?"

"Maybe," Peter said. "What if we let them run, go to wherever they're going, then send the information to the local police?"

"That could work," Jefferson nodded. "They won't act on the information, as they'd have no jurisdiction over the crimes here, but they'd certainly keep an eye on them. Soon as they put a foot in the wrong place, they'd be picked up. If they've gone far enough away, the boss will never hear about their incarceration. They'd be free to either live their lives quietly or serve their sentence, depending on what choices they make in the future."

"That sounds like the best option. Their future is in their own hands—based on their own choices—and not down to us. I've got one more question though. Jefferson, do you really think this will work? Will they run, or will they just come after us in a big way? If they eliminate the threat, they can carry on as before, right?"

"It's a possibility you can't rule out. I'd make sure that your little note informs them there are various copies of the information, and if anything happens to any of you that isn't obviously natural causes, several lawyers have instructions on where to send the information. It's an insurance policy, but it isn't a fail-safe. I don't suppose any of you are armed, just in case?"

Several members of the group looked horrified at the suggestion, and Jefferson had his answer. "I guess not then. Well, we'll just have to hope this works. Get the package ready, then one of you drop it at the coffee shop, come right back, and stay together. I'll be watching for it being picked up and will follow its trail. Once it's in Sal's hands, I'll tail him and see what he does. With a bit of luck, he'll head for the nearest airport. Best I can do is give you the heads up if it looks like they're not going to run or if they head in this direction. I'd be hot on their heels, of course, but we don't know how many Sal has in his pocket."

Jefferson rose to leave, handing back everything he had borrowed for the investigation and everything he'd managed to add to it. He went around the room, shaking hands as everyone thanked him for his assistance.

"Good luck, guys. I'll be in touch."

With a growl, then a roar of his Harley, he disappeared.

"Okay then, folks," Carter said with a worried frown. "It's crunch time. Carrie, are you feeling up to pitching in with Chelsea, Kade, and Antonio to word the letter while Chelsea duplicates the stills and the rest of the info?"

"I'm not sure," she replied, pale-faced and sweating. "I don't feel so good; I might be fine in twenty minutes or so if I lie down."

"What's wrong, Carrie?" Grace asked, rushing over to her daughter's side.

"It's nothing. I'm just feeling a little light-headed and queasy. I'm sure I'll be okay with a glass of water and a lie down."

Maggie went to fetch the water while Grace helped Carrie to her feet. "Come and lie down in my room. No point in going over to the other house."

The family looked worriedly at each other as they departed. "I think the stress of the situation is getting to her," Carter said. "Let's see if we can get everything done; maybe she'll sleep through the rest, and it'll all be over by the time she wakes up. Antonio, if you'd rather sit with her—"

"Grace will stay with her for now. She'll let me know if I'm needed. I'll check on her in half an hour or so. Let's get started."

The team got to work, with Peter contacting several lawyers to give them instructions, ensuring nothing in the package was going to be a lie except for their intention to release the information further. Even those with no further part to play for the moment didn't rejoin the harvest—they were too anxious.

***

It was 1 pm before they got the first call they had been waiting for. Carter had taken the package to the coffee shop and delivered it as instructed mid-morning. They had all been on pins and needles since his return. They were gathered in the kitchen while the women were cleaning up from lunch, keeping each other company and trying to take their minds off what might transpire in the very near future. The only family members missing were Carrie, who at last check had been fast asleep, and Antonio, who was sitting by her side, keeping an eye on her and waiting to see how she felt when she woke up. Carter glanced around at the pinched faces before answering the call, then took and exhaled a deep breath.

"Package is in the main man's hands. I'll keep you posted," was all Jefferson said before he hung up. Carter relayed the message to the others, who simply stared at each other, not knowing what to say. Very soon, they would find out if all their planning would work or if the course of their lives was about to be drastically altered. None of them had expected to be walking this particular path when they answered the call for help from Carter, but they accepted it as something they had to do, whatever the outcome. They all tried to relax in the living room, chatting inanely about the harvest and other matters that seemed trivial in the grand scheme of events about to go down. Phones were programmed to dial 9-1-1 at the touch of a button.

It took over three hours before the phone rang again, and Carter answered it nervously. If something bad was going to happen at the house, he didn't want the unsuspecting students to be anywhere near the place, but if events hadn't played out by sundown, they would all be directly outside the house for dinner. It was a complication they really didn't need. Putting the phone to his ear, he listened carefully.

Hanging up, he collapsed heavily into one of the over-stuffed chairs, putting his head in his hands.

"It didn't work, did it?" Cassie asked miserably. "What did I miss?"

"Nothing, Sis. You missed absolutely nothing," Carter replied, standing up and going over to hug his sister. "It just all caught up with me for a second there. Jefferson watched Sal make several calls on his cell phone on the way to his house. He came back out with two carry-all bags and made several stops around the city, taking one bag with him each time.

Jefferson said it was getting heavier each time he vacated a place to return to his car. In other words, they've gathered up all their cash people were holding for them. The four men he recognized from the video are now all on a flight into Mexico City International Airport. He's got a contact watching the other end, making sure they get off that plane and tracking their movements from there. He'll keep us updated, but he told us we've got nothing else to worry about—they're definitely running and not intending to come back. It's over, everyone!"

The family whooped and cheered, even the stoic Nigel giving in to the relief of the moment. Hugs were exchanged all round, and even some tears were shed.

"I can't thank you all enough," Kate said, relief making her tear up. "Oh, my goodness, you've all been so wonderful! You have no idea how much this means to me," she said through her sobs, hugging Carter. He lifted her off her feet and swung her around exuberantly, placing her back on her feet before kissing her deeply, much to the delight of their audience.

"What's going on?" said a groggy voice at the base of the stairs.

The group turned to see a sleepy, tousled Carrie standing there, Antonio behind her with a protective hand on her shoulder.

"How are you feeling?" Carter asked. "Do you need anything?"

"I'm feeling much better, and all I need is an explanation for all this rowdiness."

"Cassie's plan worked! They're leaving. They gathered up their ill-gotten gains and are heading for Mexico."

"You mean I slept through everything? Absolutely everything?"

"Pretty much. Jefferson's having them tailed at the other end and will inform us of their final destination, but other than that, you missed it all."

Carrie groaned in mock despair. "They're not even born yet, and already these little darlings are making sure I'm missing out on things," she said, affectionately rubbing her ever expanding tummy.

"Welcome to parenthood," Grace laughed. "You'd better get used to it—you've got at least twenty-one years of it to go."

Chapter Nineteen

Carter and Kate sat outside in the sunshine. It seemed like forever since the two of them had been alone together.

"So what happens now?" Kate asked.

Courtney, Peter, Chelsea, and Kade had left the previous day, claiming they had to get back to work now that they knew everyone was safe and there were more than enough hands working on the vineyard. Cassie had gone with them, and Nigel had accompanied her, saying someone needed to be around on the homestead to keep an eye on her alone in the guesthouse. After her recent experiences, Cassie hadn't refused his offer or argued the point.

Kate had invited them to come and stay anytime, in particular for the parties at the end of the harvest. They had all promised they would try. Antonio and Carrie had said they would like to stay a while longer, finally having that relaxing holiday they had been promised, and Maggie and Grace had said they were still needed to run the house and feed the workers so Kate could work the harvest, determined not to leave Carrie's side.

Kate had received one last letter from the mobsters—Joshua's marker, with the words "settled in full" written across it. Everyone doubted they would hear from them ever again. They had shacked up in some small town in Mexico, and according to Jefferson's sources, they had been keeping their noses clean so far. His contact there had a copy of the package to hand over to local authorities if that situation ever changed.

Carter twirled his glass of orange juice around on the table in front of him. "You know, I've been doing a lot of thinking and a lot of praying since this was all wrapped up. Now that the gambling debt isn't hanging over your head, you should be able to get this place back on its feet."

"Yes, the small payments I've been able to make against the arrears and the projected figures from this years' production have been enough for the bank to renegotiate the terms of the loan. The income from the guest house will certainly help too as business picks up through the harvest and after. It'll take a while, but I think we'll be able to claw our way out of the hole we were in."

"That's good."

"It's more than good, it's amazing! Josh and I are so grateful, even if he doesn't know the half of everything you did. You saved us, Carter. You saved everything—our home, our business, even our lives. We couldn't have survived without you. There just aren't enough words to thank you."

"It wasn't all me. I couldn't have done it without the help of the whole family."

"Yes, but their love for you was what brought them here, what made them rally around us and get involved. They all contributed to our survival. If you and I hadn't met up that day in San Francisco, I dread to think where Josh and I would be right now."

"Things happen how they're supposed to happen, Kate. I was meant to be there that day, and I was meant to make the decisions I did, bringing everyone to you, even accidently. It was our path to walk, and no doubt everything we learned through this will affect other aspects of our lives."

"I guess we're all a little different than we used to be."

"Perhaps we are," Carter smiled, then paused. "Kate, I've been thinking about your offer to stay."

"You're going to refuse, aren't you?"

"Yes and no. I'm going to pop back for a few days and check up on some of my projects that have been put into the hands of others during my absence. Then I'm coming back to stay until the end of the harvest, but after that, I have to return to my office."

Tears filled Kate's eyes. "I understand," she whispered, dropping her head to hide her sorrow. He did, after all, have a job, and other people depended on him, too.

"No, you don't understand, because I wasn't finished yet," Carter said, reaching out and lifting her chin with his finger. "When I get there, Im going to give my boss notice. I have to finish the projects I committed to, and that could take maybe six to eight months, but after that, if you're agreeable, I'd very much like to build my own studio here on the property and start my own firm."

"This property? You mean you'd come back?" Kate barely dared to hope.

"Yes, I want to come back. In fact, I'm not so sure I'm even leaving. I could stay here while Grace and Maggie are here, although my hours are pretty crazy. The commute isn't so bad, though, and since I bought that car...."

Carter grinned as Kate threw herself into his lap and smothered his face with kisses. "Wait a minute." She pulled back, looking into his face, but didn't release her hands from his shoulders. "What happens after your family leaves?"

"One of two things. I move into the guesthouse because living in your home just wouldn't be right—not to mention too much of a temptation."

"What's the other alternative?"

"I like this one better, personally. Once the harvest is over, and all the grapes are fermenting away, we hop over to Utah and get married. Then I can move in permanently."

"But you won't be able to have a temple wedding that soon."

"I think we both want a relationship that endures throughout eternity. And I've decided God obviously has other plans for me, at least in the short-term. He led me back to you, and it's where I was always meant to be; we just needed to take a diverse route to get there. He knows what He's doing, and if I'm not meant to have a temple wedding right now, who am I to argue with Him? We'll get to the temple in our own time.

The most important thing is that I want to be with you for the rest of my life and beyond."

"Carter Carpenter, are you asking me to marry you?"

"Yes, Katherine Peterson, that's exactly what I'm doing."

Kate jumped from his lap. "Then stand up and ask me properly, you idiot."

Laughing, Carter stood, then took on a serious look as he got down on one knee in front of Kate. From his pocket, he slipped out a small burgundy box and opened it, holding it up and taking her hand as he spoke.

"Kate, I love you with all my heart and soul. I want to be by your side for eternity; nothing would make me happier than if you would say yes. Will you marry me?"

"Yes!" Kate squealed. "Yes, of course, I'll marry you! I love you too, Carter, with all my heart. You're my best friend, my partner, my soul mate, and my hero who ensured our survival. I'll love you forever."

Carter slipped the ring on Kate's finger before gathering her into his arms for a deeply passionate kiss. They were so wrapped up in one another that neither of them noticed Grace and Maggie watching from the window, smiling contentedly at each other before turning away and giving the couple their privacy.

"Looks like the end-of-harvest party will be quite the special celebration this year," said Maggie. "And you'll have a grandson soon!"

"He took his time," Grace commented. "But he got there in the end. Guess we'll need to get ready for another wedding in the family, Maggie, and little Josh around the house, too."

The women chuckled, happy to see one more member of their family settled with the love of his life.

***

Other Books in this Series

Best Seller

Sacrifice, Carries Story

The Carpenter Chronicles, Book 1

Available now in paperback and ebook.

 Click here to order book 1 of the series.

Best Seller

Sanctuary, Chelsea's Story

The Carpenter Chronicles, Book 2

Available now in paperback and ebook.

Click here to order book 2 of the series.

Best Seller

Salvation, Courtney's Story

The Carpenter Chronicles, Book 3

Available now in paperback and ebook.

Click here to order book 3 of the series.

Other Books by Janice Limb Myers

Click the links below to view the book pages on Amazon.

1. Hunter Becomes a Pirate

2. Carolee Sings in the Christmas Choir: A Christmas Story for Children of All Ages

3. Carolee Canta en el Coro Navideño - Una Relato Navideño para Niños de Todas las Edades

4. Rachel's Little Quote Book: Messages She Left Us

If you've enjoyed reading this book, I'd like to ask a favor of you. Will you please leave some positive feedback on the Amazon sales page for it so other readers will know you liked it. It will really help get our Christian message out and I would so, so appreciate it.

Just click here!

For updates on coming releases, and discount pricing for books by Janice Limb Myers, please sign up here:

http://JaniceLimbMyers.com

Support Christian Authors and Read Great Books:
Christian Books in Multiple Genres, Join Christian Indie Author ~ Readers Group on Facebook for opportunities to learn about other great Christian authors.
https://www.facebook.com/groups/291215317668431/

www.ingramcontent.com/pod-product-compliance
Lightning Source LLC
Chambersburg PA
CBHW070816180626
46818CB00001B/291